I0710077

WORKBOOK PRESS LLC
187 E Warm Springs Rd
Suite B285 Las Vegas NV 89119 USA

Website: https://workbookpress.com/
Hotline: 1-888-818-4856
Email: admin@workbookpress.com

Ordering Information:
Quantity sales. Special discounts are available on quantity purchases by corporations, associations, and others. For details, contact the publisher at the address above.

ISBN-13:   978-1-963718-84-3 Paperback Version
                978-1-963718-85-0 Digital Version

PUB. DATE: 07/19/2024

GUANAJA CHRONICLES

MODERN DAY WAR
FOR THE BAY ISLANDS

PROFESSIONAL CARIBBEAN SCUBA
THE STARR RESORT. GUANAJA

LANCE STARR

BOOK TWO

CHAPTER ONE

Sites of Passion and Intrigue

The weather surrounding the owner's bungalow on Guanaja in the Caribbean was not hot although seriously warm with never ending humidity. A/C was quietly humming inside. Down the hill in the kitchen/restaurant on the path to the dive ramp boats, the cook and assistant were trying to organize breakfast without waking the boss, me. I had awakened to the sound of the lapping surf and the light breath of my Vanna at my shoulder. We didn't have a dive group until tomorrow, so no need to rise early.

I rolled over to doze for a while longer and my hand flowed gently down her side. Her blond hair shivered around her breasts. My touch raised a single bump; she didn't wake. Her lovely closed green eyes hid the constant energy she evinced every waking moment. She and I were co-owners of the resort, seconded as needed by Roberto Fernandez, a Honduran I had first met in the University Dorm. I had gone to Honduras with him for Spring break while others went to Miami. He'd had enough beer with me and my room-mate to know my dreams, and I his. On this trip with his father supervising, he bought a reef shrimp farm and dolphin riding show. To be developed after graduation and a trip across Europe, he didn't get past Spain.

They also had scouted this island, Guanaja, for the Lance Starr Resort for advanced Scuba Diving. A foreigner buying land in a country faces a momentous challenge. In a country fighting daily against several drug cartels with fingers polluting all levels of government, it was torture. The fact Roberto's Dad had been in government service for years before the cartels, gave me the good luck to buy it at all. Roberto had power of attorney for any window dressing in the ownership documents. It was not the operating understanding of the enterprise. He was a diver, shrimp, not tourists. He backed me in short term emergency, or when I had to go to Frankfurt for Mercedes. It was the genius of my college room-mate, Greg, along with my degree in metals and plastics allowing me to develop the resort. A patent pay-out from Mercedes for a futuristic dash board saved me from bankrupting my parents. Greg imagined, I designed.

I quietly watched Vanna sleep, "my cup" in Jim Neighbors words, "overflowing with love". She was as lovely with them closed as she was fiery and caring with them blazing.

We avoided any nostalgia for her horrors faced in saving my life four times in skirmishes with the Cartel. I had returned the favor, but the speed, judgment and accuracy were hers.

As she was flickering, I slipped away. She'd make no negative response to a morning kiss. Given the chance, I'd lead with something minty and sweet.

At seventeen, I dated three girls: One Return to School Dance, one Homecoming, and finally, Prom. The second told me on her doorstep my kiss was a candy cane. Oh, so foolish and naïve, I invited someone else to the third dance. The following year the girl who had complemented my kiss had moved and I never saw her again. Until this day I never prepare to go on a date, I think of her. I seldom fail to 'mint up'.

In our little cabana, there was no reason to hurry. I had to cool because the sheet, the only covering we needed, was pretty much nowhere to be seen over her. I heard a humble moan and a slap as she tried to locate me in the bed.

"Where are you?"

"Cleaning up."

"Lance, I wish I could make feeling you the first thing I do in the morning, come back!"

"Be careful what you wish for."

"Get back here and I will show you what I wish for."

Dressed in the minimum for an excited guy, I emerged from the doorway, satisfied her instincts, and left with a sweet wisp of mint.

It was sweet; not simple. Vanna is a woman five inches shorter than me. She has flowing blond hair and deadly green eyes speaking tons, wherever. As I sit on the edge of the bed, she moves in and I wrap my arms around her hips, erotic flicks where she is pleasantly shaven. Delightful, exploring her thighs drives new sensations. Along those miles, she is soft, warm, and slippery. Squeeze, and you find a firm, iron-like underpinning. She is a diver, a lifesaver, and honed as a Navy Seal. To have such a woman wishing for me in the morning, stops my breath. Frivolous with me as I splash, usually too soon, roaring two, three, four, more times sharing her OWN, is my heaven on earth.

CHAPTER TWO

The Conflict

After the mauled wardrobe, we went down to the bar/ restaurant. The local scuba ramp boat captains were there with Josh, a new professional diver/businessman. He replaced Trey. Trey fell in love with the owner of a pizza restaurant who brought her volunteer fire department for ten days of diving. After giving the two week contractual notice and fighting his final Cartel skirmish, he went back to her.

Bacon served up hot, as forks raised, the camp sea-band radio crackled. The window identified radio call name: Octavio. Rayban Hernandez, captain and owner of the Octavio, a combo commercial fisherman and deep sea fishing tour cruiser, responded.

This could be good news or very bad news. Food back in the oven, we hurried to the top of the resort where radar, sensors and a drone were always minutes from activation.

The usual marauders were radicalized Cartel drug minions, occasionally a White Supremacist trying to refill the treasury of which the previous club officers had absconded. Today, we located Octavio; no other bogies.

"Birdcage, this is Octavio, over. Do you read me, Birdcage?"

We had been involved for some time with Octavio being attacked by these same pirates, sometimes to beat him up, and sometimes to steal his catch and take it in their boats up to Gulfport wholesale markets. There was a four hour trip usually involved for Octavio. Unfortunately it had to pass west in attack range of the pirate rats located on Roaban. This, the largest, infested of the Bay Islands.

With the support of Captain Brearly of the huge, mobile island neighborhood moored on Roaban, we had ridden shotgun for Rayban. We reduced pirate attack success, often with much thug life lost, or sunk.

Our protection took the form of the Blue-Coats in the Revolutionary War. Large cartels with radicalized thugs, and the country's army controlled by the Cartel against the few of us. This was the only way we could protect our livelihoods.

We look for weaknesses and capitalize on them. At the same time, leave no evidence of our operations; including all implements and, oh so ugly, remains of killers.

Roberto and his father were having trouble with the shrimp farm. They went to the local police for help; laughed out of their offices. The Cartel was paying officials at all levels. Son and Dad went to country mainland courts with no success. To the highest levels in the country, paid off. Rumored with money shared for campaigns of Southern Senators of the U.S.

There was no law enforcement nor court order to bring justice to this sick organizational collapse. On the other hand, I had several hundreds of thousands invested in a life/business here. Roberto did as well. The mobile Island was affected occasionally. If their extremely wealthy board of directors lost patience, the response was thunder personified.

CHAPTER THREE

Neighbors

Rayban, call name Octavio, a single operator of a business here had to depend on friends and neighbors for assistance. We provided!

"Octavio, we have you 5X5. Are you ok, what's happening?"

"Birdcage, we are fine and making good headway. I wondered if you would check your long-ranging radar to see if any threats are developing."

Lance responded, "Octavio, I checked all sources including the drone on your call. Nothing developing at the moment. Now we know you are on the waves, we'll keep an eye out. Run flank speed for two hours and I will check again. If things are clear, I will tuck in against Vanna and you can back off to three bells. If not, I will call. Good sailing, Birdcage out."

We returned to breakfast, a mourner for desert, and down to the dock to clean and prepare for the next day.

Octavio had a mom and younger brother living in a village called Sambo Creek on the north coast. Most of the inhabitants were the offspring of the slave boats coming from Africa. Decades before they blew south and foundered on the reefs of the Caribbean. He was coming up on thirty years old with one of the most lucrative businesses on the coast. He wasn't married, nor even dating much. Friends kidded him and chided him. Nothing developing.

The thugs too frequently frustrated him launched from Roaban Island heading north-east where he was running northwest toward Gulfport. They'd celebrate if they ever could rob him and push him into the Atlantic.

Octavio was going to dock, wholesale flounder this time, east of the bayous of the south coast. There was a good number of outlaws in there I worried might someday join up with the Mafia Don. J Mondo.

CHAPTER FOUR

Vanna and Zulinda: Sparks!

With the new tourists in mind, I asked Vanna to call Zulinda, owner of the "Unclad. Com" resort south on the island. Before Vanna arrived at the resort and became my love and co-operator, Zulinda and I had joined forces against cartel pirates sinking or stealing our supplies from Cuenca. We needed a joint supply run.

Zulinda modeled the behavior she expected of her clients, and wore nothing. No thong, nothing! We sent two boats, or one, with two guys running shotgun and the problem was resolved. The woman was a 6' 5" grey/blue eyed wonder. I had seen her in the distance when we were building Starr. I had never gone over, knowing reactions come forth quite expectedly.

Zulinda had been running her camp three years before I began to build mine. Eventually, we talked about our similar business problems once per month. I, fully dressed; she thread-less. Business and survival on the island occupied our minds and the relationship smoothed out to be warm, supportive, but platonic.

Vanna came and she and I bonded, fiercely. Vanna knew the timeline of camp development and on the day Zulinda first arrived, in the nothing-at-all, Vanna reflected on my hunger for herself. She assumed what I could be with her, I'd be with the striking beauty Zulinda.

Assumed! I was not without a woman several times building camp, not Zulinda. The Fifth Amendment on any others, but Vanna went to the changing room of the cabana, undressed and chose to compete nude to nude. Vanna went after Zulinda with burning eyes. Verbal, but viscous. I moved aside. Eventually it ended. Zulinda tried to heal the feelings, Things were only on hold.

Zulinda shamed Vanna for her assumptions and pointed out which man she was actually concerned about in the upcoming self-defense raid: Rayban Hernandez.

Zulinda left and I took Vanna to the bedroom to sooth her feelings.

It was cool for the night. Vanna settled and morning was hot. Almost delayed the trip. We hurried off together to prepare our counter-attack if endangered.

If inter-camp meetings were needed or joint supply trips, or any little, tiny thing developed between camps, I sent Vanna exclusively.

CHAPTER FIVE

A Turn-Around On The Way Back

The dive clubs came in on the six-seater Cessnas from Cuenca to a gravel airport on a nearby island. It served Unclad.com and the Starr Professional Diving Camp. We had the two ramp diving boats and another security high speed coast guard type craft. We took four trips to get clients to the pier and belongings to ramp boats, or cabanas. The group had one woman. I had specifically searched for a woman camp co-operator and was glad to have Vanna here. Temporary for now but apt to contracted in the near future. Of course, more for other reasons. There were 28 total guests so we used both ramp boats and boat captains.

After dinner, I spoke with all guests reminding them of underwater hand-signing and camp response to any damage to the reef. "Take only pictures and leave only bubbles." They had a morning and afternoon dive available daily and a night dive on Wednesdays depending on weather. Northerners, our signature storm typically developed at sun-down, full force before we knew it.

The next morning, we decided to send Vanna in the boat with the other woman, and our diver/administrator Josh with the other men and captain.

With Octavio in Gulfport, which we expected to be two nights, I went with a boat captain and one of Zulinda's staff, dressed and well-armed, to Cuenca for supplies. Depending on weather we might get the two, two-hour trips in one day. Northerners concerned us. On this day, while loading supplies, one hit the coast. We had to unload and get into a hotel. Anticipating the camp arrivals, we left very early the following day and had the cook re-stocked and bubbling well before the third and final flight.

I scanned to locate Octavio on his way following the storm. There was no Octavio anywhere. I was hopeful he had found a date to last overnight for a change. I went to my now lonely bungalow and lay for a snooze. No sooner had I closed my eyes, the camp sea radio ramped off.

Rayban finally had a date, overnight, with a sharp girl. Returning to the port, two cartel thug boats were stalking him. He headed for the east exit of Gulfport and they'd followed. West they'd followed again.

Lance with sleep in his eyes, "This is Birdcage, what's wrong Octavio?" Lance paused to listen. "Ok, Octavio. Go back among the yachts. If you know anybody there, stay and chat with them. At least don't get out of the breakwater. Hold on, Octavio."

Lance radios, "Roberto, where are you?"

"I encouraged some shrimp relationship building and Cindy had a better idea. Why are you interrupting me?"

"Roberto, I'm sorry, my shame to Cindy. Listen to this conversation with Octavio in Gulfport:"

From Lance, "How many thug boats are hunting you? Is there something they want on the boat, or will they steal the boat? Do you have the cash on board from the flounder sales? Do you have armament? Good, Octavio, keep it absolutely out of sight. If cops there see a big black guy with an RPG, I'll be hunting for bail money. Better, get a sound suppressed rifle with regular ammo. One sec., I've got Roberto."

"Guys, I put all cash in a safe deposit in Gulfport for my lawyer Felipe to deal with. They are going to take my boat only over my dead body. I can out-run them. I got 23 knots to their seven."

"Octavio, at ease! Songbird, the U.S. Drone base told me he saw them cruising at 18 knots with an empty boat. Roberto is on his way to me. We (Birdcage) will come part of the way for you. Don't run until I tell you we are in position! Only then do you make a run for us. I will call the timing. Understood? Only if they make a move to come inside the breakwater do you start shooting and running. Clear?"

"Well, you've always been right before. Put your boat in overdrive on hot. I am sweating it here! Octavio, out"

CHAPTER SIX

Pirates Don

"Octavio, Roberto should be here in a half hour. Remember, my security craft can run over 33 knots. Octavio, don't depend on the U.S. Coast Guard. They will have to request orders from up a chain where these Texas congress' payoffs may already be in the bank. Their response, among others, bartered by mafia, Don J: to lie and screw with you. By the time help arrives, if at all, you'd be destroyed. Don't trust even a black cop if he is decked out in gold chains. He'll be on somebodies payroll. I may sound a disloyal, chagrinned American but in the last five years, the worst has always become reality from the hog to the complicit Re-s."

"Vanna, where are you in the dive, over?"

"Birdcage, only the pros have more than five minutes air left. We're boarding over half of the clients. What can I do, over?"

"Vanna, we don't want to spook the divers. Get the pros early if you can. Take a slow turn back to the dock and floor it. I need you there quickly to get the drone up, green laser. Get us on radar. Call when you are set, over."

Vanna, "Roger, out!"

"Octavio, be there soon. Put your suppressed arms close at hand, out of sight. If you actually need to shoot, use them so authorities or crooks can't locate the source. I see Roberto In the distance, Birdcage Out."

An hour later with Lance's big Chevy inboard whining, the

distance had been closed only to half. Lance radioed Captain Brearly on the mobile island. He had his big drone, Black Bird, up too far away. There are no dependable U.S. rules of engagement here. We needed to get the meeting outside of U.S. waters and away from any Coast Guard 'authorized' involvement. Their Rules of Engagement would kill us.

"Flank speed, NOW, Octavio", barked Vanna."

Octavio hammered his cruiser out of the East breakwater heading west of south. The thugs were surprised, maneuvered after him losing a minute and a half. They were up to 18 knots with Octavio at 23, he was not making needed separation. Armament from the thugs could cover the distance.

"With Roberto, I had my Chevy screaming and was, with wind direction, heading North-West to Rayban at 35 knots. If Vanna's calculations and sea currents cooperated, Roberto and I could thread the needle between the rogues and Octavio with the distance of 200 meters each side."

Roberto slipped below and brought out the armament. Three sound suppressed rifles with the first volleys dark, and the second two with tracers. Two RPG's and four subsurface torpedoes.

Octavio had even more lethal weapons; but in choppy waters had trouble shooting accurately.

Lance orders, "Octavio, we're between you and your attackers. You have no assistant. Get low, full speed, and let us do the shooting."

"Birdcage, Vanna said, I'm here. Fully locked and loaded. Orders?"

"Vanna, Roberto has two torpedoes in the water, port and starboard of us. Get them on your drone scope. Bring some fire immediately on the port boat since their rifles are getting awfully close to me. You can use the yellow lens. I'll stall the starboard rifle fire. If Roberto misses either thug boat, green lens either or both until it sinks. Anything left, I will take out with the Holland and Holland with four power scope. Copy?"

Octavio stutters, "Birdcage, I've got a bazooka. Let me defend my boat! Out!"

"Octavio, come back, stay down. Roberto is arming the torpedoes. If he doesn't take both boilers out in the next minute, Vanna will laze them out. If that fails, you can pop your head and use whatever you have aboard. Do not use the bazooka unless it is absolutely the last option to save your boat. The thunder and flash will be unmistakable even from Gulfport. Do you copy?"

"Copy birdcage, my stop watch is running."

"Roberto, send a torpedo each way. If you sense a miss, go hard with double taps. The rogues are not hiding below their gunwales. Shoot bogies or the bottom of their boilers to the port side."

Roberto's torpedo hit the port thug boat solid in the boiler. Two flailing bodies rocketed up and away. With his tracers, he hit them both before they hit to drown if they weren't already gone.

Vanna quickly switched to the starboard thugs where I had been suppressing fire and it was not sinking. She green-lazed the flame hoses on the boiler and it whammed all parts and all thugs to decimation. We inspected the area for any remnants of our action. It was clear Octavio would get home safely tonight.

CHAPTER SEVEN

Breather

We escorted Octavio south until we saw Guanaja on the starboard side. He continued to Sambo under the eyes of our radar and drone.

It was after midnight with full moon as we moored the security craft to our dock. Camp lights were on generator as normal and all tent lights were out. Some interesting snoring. Our luck was holding; we had been able to deal with the Cartel without worrying our important guests, our best "word of mouth" advertising. Josh and another boat captain took both daytime dives the next day.

CHAPTER EIGHT

Discussion With Brearly And Work Trip To Frankfurt

After our day of purported rest, we both took the group morning dive trips. Divers had viewed the wall a mile off the north coast and today would explore the shallower, more colorful reef to the east of the island. Vanna and I were now taking pressure off the captains because in two weeks we'd be going to Frankfurt for two or more months. It was still more busy hours for the full time captains. We took the Wednesday night dives as well. Our itineraries for divers were intense, and not for novices unless booked in advance with accompanied trainers. Diving the whole itinerary seldom happened for all visitors. The recent exception had been the Mukwonago Volunteer Fire Dept. team of twelve, who ultimately absconded with Trey. Or Fran did! They didn't miss a breath of any dive day or night.

CHAPTER NINE

Familiarization

Vanna and I made a point of taking the night dives for three weeks before any travel. Again, she was a delightful exception to any rules. She'd do Monday and Tuesday, both dives and the Wednesday night without missing a beat. When I wasn't expecting it, she was apt to do me any given Wednesday night after the dive. This week was not the exception but we were taking the first Thursday dive.

A choppy surf vibrated stiff knees for me while Vanna was making "poor, poor boy faces" at me from the other ramp boat. Stiff or not, it was a joy to see her teasing the seduction.

We knew our flora and fauna very well. Everybody got as close as they could to the moray eel. They saw only the sand in the water behind the ray who slept here. We had visitors under the pier as well. Two squid flashed to deep water every day, and a rock fish hung around. Step on the thorn of one of these and worse than an allergy, you'd be down for days or more.

CHAPTER TEN

Brearly's Concerns After Octavio's Curious Attack

We did the two morning dives the following Thursday because Captain Brearly had asked us to a late lunch. There was no doubt in my mind about the discussion. We took the security boat for the 20 minute ride, depending on wind, to the huge neighborhood he led. Big smiles Maria, on a luscious Mrs. Brearly body welcomed us on the dock. She was a bronze tanned woman with roots a couple of generations back in Costa Rica. We'd heard the story of the Captain's capture of this university grad-beauty a few years ago. Educated women around these islands were few in number. The Cartel ignored any law and killed any enforcement for the trafficked.

Maria stored her 300 Weatherby with the security captain. She escorted us to the six block Captain's tower and quarters. Time for a drink imported to the island, not available even at my upscale resort. The invited minute lunch, more a dinner, was served.

Brearly was in his dress whites, clear why Maria let him catch her. His face showed some concern, nothing other than our Germany and his desire for a leave with Maria to his home culture, came up. A double Bailys was desert and Maria called in the housekeeper to clear. Vanna got a peck from Maria who floated off somewhere. Brearly, front and center, would give her a full debriefing on her pillow tonight. She was intellectually much more than a north coast bed-warmer.

He said, "I heard some noticeable popping and banging the other night. Sound travels fast from Gulfport over the water.

I saw you escorting Octavio later. Is he ok, any damage to his lovely cruiser?"

Vanna quickly answered, "summarizing the actions."

"Brearly", with an endearing smile for Vanna, said Lance, "something here is wrong. We have cooperatively defended some lives and property. Every skirmish has initiated from the North Coast near SPS or the other side of Orilla Island. What generated something on the doorway of the Gulfport Marina?"

Vanna recounted what happened. I added we kept the skirmish well off-shore to avoid any blowback from a harbormaster.

Lance continued, "But, why, stumps me. I was hoping your board might have something. The only anomaly other than theft is the common thread of trying to force Octavio toward the east. If we have a west wind pushing him closer to the north of you, or Orilla, their efforts are more nefarious to push him east. The drone picked up that slight deviation. I missed it completely. Octavio had nothing of value on the craft other than the craft itself. His cash goes in a bank downtown Gulfport and his lawyer keeps track of how he can reduce taxes, and avoid most of them from this scam government. Even his assistant wasn't there. That, he may want to re-think."

CHAPTER ELEVEN

Reconnaissance

21

Brearly ponders, "Lance, my corporation has been snooping around very gingerly to see what we are facing, the core center group or individual sending out these raids. I expect knowledge by the end of the year, possibly U.S. Senatorial elections driven. I can't promise it will be actionable information. If you volunteer, you might escort well, and very well, Octavio, to the port north of SPS. Go secretly, heavily armed in your two fastest boats. Take Vanna! Do nothing if you can avoid it; observe as long as you can. I know I've interfered with hours of sleep in your mind, but I can't say more."

Brearly and two armed securty escorted us to our security boat at which point he left us and the security people drove along in a boat accompanying us back to our dock.

We monitored Octavio's trips to Gulfport for two additional weeks. There were no anomalies and I had to get back to Frankfurt. As always, Roberto hovered about Starr Resort and skyped weekly.

CHAPTER TWELVE

Frankfurt

The first month in Germany was hurried with the design and construction of various Mercedes components. I did reverse-engineering training and forward training with new ideas Greg kept rolling down his pike. Vanna kept herself busy with shopping, every night meeting me with devil's eyes. Finally I gave up on guessing. The runway upon eventual return to Guanja would be breathtaking.

After the intense month on the continent, I had a three week break before receiving parts tied up in the Suez Canal. We had talked our last trip of visiting Austria. We had time and the climate was tolerable. We trained to Munich, borrowed Greg's Mercedes and headed for Salzburg. It was only a half day from Munich through humungous mountain passes. I was glad we had passed on our idea earlier because a snow-slide could wipe us out.

Heavy wooden planks and dirndl wall hangings put us directly in the culture. The room with bed and couch was floating with soft comforters and carved erotic ceilings.

We were full; did a pre-bubble. Thanks to Brearly, I was nightly trying to project what problem his people were pursuing in SPS. We were scanning the Caribbean from west to east, checking out coastlines, any other shipping, any danger to the banana industry, a giant there. From Western Florida on through southern Texas, control of behavior regarding guns, attitudes toward federal government, and healthcare were torture on the sick or elderly. They even had their own electric grid which couldn't be attached to the national in case of local outages. Pay their own costs rather than taxes and be responsible for their own maintenance. Recent outages had brought the inadequacy to country-wide recognition. One of their southern Senators was so indifferent he went on vacation while the people who were continually fools to vote for him suffered cold, heat, and water access. Speculation among world-aware people were he was personally receiving illegal campaign money. Older citizens paid with deaths. We could go around and around on this but spied a bottle of Kirshwasser on the mini-bar. Two shots each, and under the thick comforters we basked in local "lieben". Very culturally sensitive!

CHAPTER THIRTEEN

Pacho Mantanya

GUATAMALTECO father, Pacho was born in Managua, Nicaragua. There his name was Montanya, or mountain. He was brightest of three siblings, street smart. Eventually under the tutorship of Cartel recruiters, he became the epitome of Evil Street smart. The second echelon of the Mondo in the country met him and knew what they could do with him. They avoided giving him any idea of history.

In the ten years following, he moved up the ladder through training in fighting, shooting, water boarding and beheading. They had him watch the right TV and he became a slippery, "buddy, buddy", guy of the worst villains. He experienced directly the use of his grisly skills. He could sell ice cubes to Eskimos.

At sixteen, they bought him a wife and in three years they had three children. At 20, they bought him a green card. They moved him to a Spanish Speaking manufacturing neighborhood in Texas. Time for pay back!

CHAPTER FOURTEEN

Bloody Reset

Ceasrito's Mafia brute father had been dead for over a year and a half. Alicia had now seen two further "Don J. "Mondos" deflowered with no ramifications to her, husband Ceasrito, or their veterinary business. She watched Ceasrito carefully, closely and from afar. Their marriage was going as she drove it. She was magnetic and Ceasrito was in awe of her beauty. She controlled him as women have the armament to do. He was a guy with terrific memory but no analytical skills. She had it all. What he also had was a body of ripple and eyes entranced by her completely. His loving was intense and to see his eyes adoring her each morning was a priceless start to the day.

The reason she watched him closely was he had been son of the dead mafia Don J who had estranged him from the family. Forcing him to do disgusting Cartel tasks was relieved by four years of university. Perhaps low analysis skills contribute to an innocent mind. Home, He was a different person and soon Alicia was guiding his morals and values. They lived together for a while as Alicia tried on her new shoes before buying them.

The lightning of degenerate Mafia filth hit when a lieutenant of the Mondo took Ceasrito from his home and forced him fighting to an arena in the center of the town.

Don J barked, "Now I will make you a man who contributes to this organization. Bring in the insolent lout who teases me nights on TV and demeans my leadership."

Ceasrito tried to shake off the lieutenant and another joined in pinning him to the wall. The corpulent Mondo strutted to the center of the arena, raised his arm, looked to the wooden door and walked to the edge of the seats. A man in chains was dragged out, pulled to a log in the center of the ring. head thrust down, rolled right to Ceasrito who saw the moving grimaces.

Ceasrito ripped his arms from the lieutenants and ran to the nearest bathroom completely losing it. He ran out of the arena down to the beach and ran from vomit to vomit until he was empty. He didn't want to involve or describe any of this to Alicia but couldn't stop from seeking her solace. She took him in empathy soon offering his deepest desire.

CHAPTER FIFTTEEN

Marriage Preferred Sans Step-Anything

Ceasrito removed himself from any other Cartel horrors. She decided the marriage was due. Alicia wondered to her father, well-grounded of the horrors here, whether she could safely stay in this marriage. Speaking with his years of observation he said, "The Cartel will not attack the son of a Mondo, or immediate family, nor destroy the only business where the boy has the horsepower to succeed."

"Do I need a security guard?"

"At the moment, no. I will check sources over time if my opinion changes. Take him for a healing honeymoon over to Guatamala to dusty Antigua. Behind the clay walls, you will find quality local entertainment. Somewhere at least away from here."

I took him and with ecstasy rebuilt him for intense loyalty. He passed some exhilarating tests. I informed him to start a baby. With his dad and evil paid trophy wife gone, we could safely have a baby. We pulled into the home driveway; I took him right down. I knew him intently as a male, and myself as a veterinary. The machinery was there; no question.

Seeing the social cruelties toward women, I decided to have a boy. Sounds a bit presupposing. With lightly acid baths, vinegar pads and by controlling C's frequency and speed, I slightly increased the overall probability of effective Y sperms. Abstaining for thirteen days caused much wailing. Completely ignored, I hit pay sperm the second month.

I am built perfectly for baking babies. I wasn't certain if I want one here. We didn't peek and my recipe charmed out an 8 pound, 8 ounce bruiser. After one loving day, my heart was no longer my own. No cartel thug unless over my dead body would touch his mind or body. For the first time my emotions ignored my father's advice. I called my Asian Language teacher at A&M. I got the contact info for the Nepali guest lecturer I had evocatively befriended before I saw the fervor in Ceasrito's eyes: LAXMAN SHRESTA

CHAPTER SIXTEEN

Into U.S. Corruption

29

Pacho was not slated to be a lowly drug runner. The Cartel's radicalizers capitalized on his elusive evil to get him into office first at the community level with Republican monies into State Government in Texas where he now had residency. They continued to groom him using Cartel money to get him a large Villa where elected betrayers of a democracy could plan their obstruction and subversion of the U.S. Government. He had a budget deep enough to take representatives and wives to Caribbean Resorts. He needed no more.

CHAPTER SEVENTEEN

Long Lasting Love?

Our small group of few against the evil-many monitored each other routinely. Octavio didn't return from Gulfport in three days, I radioed. I heard music in the background, waiting for him to get outside. I listened for a few minutes, signed off, turned, and sent Vanna into paraxioms of joy: "Nerven".

Octavio pulled up to a "preparation for offloading" dock on each arrival to Gulfport. It was one hundred meters from the conveyor. Rayban moved the Octavio to the required ramp position, noted the line-up growing to the main port fish conveyor, and decided not to face the melee. He pulled away, went down, showered and dressed for a beer on the dock closer to the shore.

On the left side on the way down, he saw a woman laying back on a sun couch with a big hat over her head. He couldn't see her face. The remainder of the view was worthwhile. He slowed, she apparently didn't notice, and he walked on. He had an imported beer and headed back. He got back on his boat and with a glance back, caught a glance in return. He moved over to the conveyor, unloaded, and headed back to Sambo.

When deep sea fishing tours are out of season, he makes usually three trips to Gulfport each week.

Big Hat was back tanning the never ending thighs as he passed up for a beer. This time they had a civil, shallow conversation in passing. He took his beer back to the cruiser and went to unload, heading back south. He checked; there were continued flash glances. He docked next to our ramp boat in Guanaja, said hello, and took Vanna firmly by the hand and hurried her up to an intense conversation. Half skipping to his boat, he left full flank back south.

After dinner and a particularly flashing bed desert, I closed bubble and asked "Vanna, what was the secret conversation with Rayban today?"

"Lance, let's keep it secret, as I promised, for a while?"

Dive groups came and went with no interruption from the Cartel. It had been so long I began to wonder. I remembered Blearly's encouragement to reconnoiter the SPS north port area.

Octavio's trips to Gulfport were lengthening with me watching to be sure he wasn't in danger. Back in the bubble, Vanna showed no concern. I wondered if maybe it was some kind of relationship I'd missed. I dozed finishing my beloved voluntary chores.

Brearly's rough voice woke me. "Birdcage, this is Black Bird. Copy?"

"Roger, I copy but a sweet dream interrupted. What's up?"

"I'm afraid you'll have to shift to nightmare. Octavio is headed north and has picked up a tail of two boats. Octavio has Junior now. You better get them up to speed. Out!"

CHAPTER EIGHTEEN

Fought With New Beginnings

I launched the drone and lit off the radar.

"Octavio, this is Birdcage. Are you aware of what I'm calling about? Over"

"Yes birdcage I have them on sea radar. I'm well-armed, with Junior by my side, and probably can outrun them. However, I have a special package to take to Sambo on the way back. Fragile! I'm concerned about the return trip. If they shadow me again, I absolutely cannot gamble. I return on day three from now. I need to have the trip go as quietly as possible. I may need to have you escort me from the breakwater up there. Will you be around? Over"

"Ok, Octavio, any changes, we'll know before you do and light off the Chevy to join you. Call me early on the day you want to create your 'Phantom Parade'. Standing bye, Birdcage."

"Octavio, out!"

It was morning nap, dunk and bubble after breakfast. "I think I know the mentoring you are giving Rayban. There's a woman enjoying his rippled shoulders and other bubblable attentions. We need to plan if his heart is set on bringing her to mama in the next week. Tell me the truth."

"Yes, Lance, it's a woman, tall he says with the other accoutrements. With abundance of shy, he hinted they are involved from top to bottom. His age, I think."

"Vanna, you should radio him the day after tomorrow and

have him say the things he needs to say to prepare, but not scare her. Be sure she has a passport and any virus tests required. We will meet him up there with the security boat and all armaments and Roberto. It should go without incident. Difficult conditions, but I don't want him to lose a "keeper" due to mistakes on our part. "Vanna, use "Birdcage Drone".

CHAPTER NINETEEN

Body Guard

Ten thousand Nepalis apply to be Gurka's. Four hundred are chosen by British recruiters after grueling activities and competitions. Applicants need a working ability in English because this is the British Gurhka Division. They are trained beyond some's endurance, but are one of the most feared fighting cadres in the world.

The traditional fighting weapon is a short curved blade sword which is called the 'Gurkha'. Modern weapons have now been added to the armory. The Gurkha is worn on every belt. Candidates must be from 17 ½ to 21 to try out. The normal term of service is 15 years with all pension and health for soldier and immediate family. The pension provides a quality salary after exchange rate, ad infinitim.

The war between the British and Argentinians raged on the Falklands; the mercenary British Gurkha unit was called up. They fight quietly in the night and shadows. Their enemies, looking at first alive, melt. The Argentinian soldiers quickly retired from the slashes in the night. Laxmi Shresta was a veteran of this conflict and others nearer Asia.

Laxmi was of the Shresta caste in Nepal. Ask any policeman his last name; it's Shresta. At the minimum age, 17 ½, he went another way. He could, in fifteen years earn a lifetime of security for his family. He already was a mountain of a man. He went among the 10,000; a British recruiter saw the look in his eye. He was a medaled soldier never losing in the 15 year life plan.

At 33, he was retired, bilingual, financially sufficient for his family, and free to seek a new life. His first goal was to renovate his family home into this century with modern appliances and ornaments. Soon, he looked further.

The suburb of Bhaktapur was a half days walk from downtown Kathmandu. Ancient monuments and statues adorned streets and central squares. Having a knowledge of both the East and the West, he saw the monument the most visited. The depth of the stones steps worn off made it clear.

There were a half dozen women with their daughters viewing; discussing seriously the meaning of the carvings. Playboy and the "Art of Loving" were not seen in this culture. The carvings were accurate and included everything a young girl of arranged marriage needed to be a good wife. In this culture, birth control methods were included. And more.

As a single man, he kept his distance and showed respect between him and the participants.

Typical at these things, foreigners not knowing the customs moved right up between him and the families. He heard English, German, French, and some oriental girls speaking something he didn't know. People's dress shouted: 'Peace Corps.'

He had seen those people and knew they tried to help people out in the villages. In town they were always interested and friendly. There was however a set of horizon blue eyes under long brown hair flashing at his. A smile, brief. There was wonderment on both sides if this could be something. Blue eyes was clearly a little older and leader of the group. She locked eyes back again as she led her group away. His eyes fired. He turned away.

He wandered around the cobblestones with one thing he couldn't delete from his mind. They were gone. He didn't know anything really in depth about them, Tracking, however, had been one of his military skills. He could surely find them.

He did find them at Casey's, one of the few places you could order a water buffalo steak with no worms nor amoebas included.

He walked to her and introduced himself. She smiled and responded. They closed the place down.

Two days later he was kitted out far more cleverly than the others to find out exactly what Peace Corps people do. He had some doubts about it and Connie challenged him to come along and see for himself. He was beholden to the British instructors who drilled his English. He focused his British accent on Connie.

There were hours debating about how to deal with cross cultural parents and families. The biggest challenge of all: Connie had been appointed head of the Peace Corps in Central American/ Caribbean operations. Marrying was tough enough, taking him away was rivers of tears. They were off to the small city of Cuenca where the office for Central America was located.

CHAPTER TWENTY

Is She A Trouper;
Can She Tolerate Life-Off Shore?

anna called Octavio the next morning to brief him on emotions he might have forgotten or hadn't had to face. She laid out a sample of the speech he should give Nerven about special conditions of our Caribe. Was she babying him? Absolutely.

Apologetically, Octavio called us from Gulfport very early the next day, the departure. "Birdcage, we are being stalked. They are hanging to the west of us. They want to drive us East, or attack. We need your help. I'm trying to make this a vacation fun-trip for Nerven. I think she gets some vibs. She's very careful to do immediately what I ask. I can't give her a Rueger without knowing how she'll handle the emotional trauma."

"Octavio, Birdcage back to you. I agree with your Rueger judgement. Keep her as far out of it as you can. Secondly, don't leave safe harbor until you see the lights of my eyes. I have armament on board for this theater of operations. I have Roberto. Vanna already has you on the drone. Her call is "Birdcage Drone". I don't see how they could ever successfully attack you. I read your questions about pushing you east and shared with Brearly. He only hints he may have info at the end of the year."

Octavio breaks in, "What is so important about Orillo Key and the west?"

Lance, "Octavio, we're not going to be asking them. If they attack, I will decimate them. If I don't succeed, Vanna will light them both up. Then you and I will sweep. Come to the lip of the break-water in 1½ one hours. Hold there until you see me. I can't let them get you between me and a cross fire with the boat docks. Don't start any firing. Wait till I wave to move out to deeper water. Birdcage, Out!"

CHAPTER TWENTY ONE

Round Trip Desecration

The largest city on the Texas coast had been hammered by a huge hurricane. To be hygienic, large parts had to be rebuilt. Garbage transportation dykes had to be rebuilt, as New Orleans had done. The large corporations balked; they didn't want to pay the taxes. Even with new Re's legislation unfairly putting the burden on the general middle class and immigrant community, their greed ran rampant, SICK! Don J., Southwest Mafia head was called. He called Pacho.

Riding high in his Rolls Royce, Pacho scanned a map and developed a plan. Nobody in government wanted to improve the plan. Nobody wanted to be associated with him in any way. He was the hitman. Eventually, he became dangerous excess baggage.

He boated down to the largest port and charted a flight to follow the coast of Mexico, past Cuba, and Merida. Destination: the southern tail of Mexico, and on to San Pedro Sula, one of the most dangerous drug centers in the world.

He contacted Border control to avoid the obvious chance of being shot down as a drug transport.

"Ah, how is my old friend, Don J. Mondo doing these days?"

An envelope changed hands along with an evil smile. No flight plan nor flight problems. He went and returned to the U.S. port, went to a strip club and spent the night. The following morning he flew the Texas coast over to the Mississippi. He followed the river north a short way and saw a group of rusting barges and noted the name of the company. He flew back to the port and had his Rolls take him home.

He had dispatched his trafficked wife and kids to cheaper lodgings and had his latest waiting for him in his hot tub. He rested most of the evening and slept well late the next day. He proceeded to study some maps and much of Delores.

He called his "friend" in the port asking him to locate, rent or buy, three, thirty five foot trawlers, war surplus with gun placements. Look for some rusted on the outside; reclaimable and stable on the inside. He visited a well-known illegal arms dealer.

"Ah, how is my old friend, Don J?"

He got on the internet and located the web site of the Mississippi barge dealer. There was none. Better yet. He called information and got the land line. Ah, there was Cartel stink in the air. Orange roses to him. He agreed to rent six months in advance, paid in full by courier coming in two days.

"Clean up three, not noticeable." I tow them with Coronado's. Include chain connections. Drivers next Wednesday.

He needed a large crew, automatic with the Asst. Capo in Alamo Heights. Anybody loyal to Capo had work. He flew to San Jose, Costa Rica and got lost in the striking love pits.

CHAPTER TWENTY TWO

To Become Expats Again

Connie and Laxmi flew to Montana where there was an American consulate not overcome by Central Americans running literally for their lives. Even married to an American, it took the better part of a year for a green card visa. Several more years needed for citizenship. He had a pension well above what they needed, Connie had savings. She wanted to get back to work, excited about her new leadership role and as a matter of feminine pride. Laxmi had been in many cultures, he faced no culture shock. What was shocking, in Honduras, they got citizenship in less than a month.

He recalled at the end of his service, his Brahmin friend Devi at Texas A&M had invited him, a veteran Gurkha as a guest speaker. He also remembered the Honduran girl there whose eyes trapped his. Never to be as he had to leave her for Nepal immediately. He did knew her dreams and had met the guy in the running for the +1. If her dream came true, she was a veterinary somewhere in Honduras. They had parted on good terms. There was no rancor when, "surprise" Connie brought Alicia home from work one day. That they already knew each other knocked the socks off Connie. A blush on Alicia. Her professor, the Brahmin, was connected. Laxmi was the one shocked to an embarrassed silence. Of course, he remembered the eyes, but there had been much more. Typically shy in temperament, he spoke little. They talked about Cesarito and the new baby, clearing the air for everybody about anybody. Laxmi relaxed and warmed up.

They worked together to prepare, uphill, for Moon Mountain. Alone, they camped; he showed his outdoor skills. He pitched the mosquito net. They shared some indoor skills! The next day they arrived by sundown. He went for first introductions. They met Connie's team. She sat them down to outline their mission.

CHAPTER TWENTY THREE

Welcome Procession to Sambo

Trying to act relaxed with Nerven, Octavio was relieved to see Lance's Chevy evolve in the distance. Lance waived him out of the breakwater and flew toward his starboard side. Rayban headed Octavio southwest, the thugs hard after him. Trying some experiments, Octavio changed to due west. Birdcage copied him. The thugs were screaming their limited vocabulary, cutting back and forth to force him south or east.

"Octavio, this is Birdcage. Now try to head due south and see what happens. We'll need distance from the breakwater if there is noise. How is Nerven doing?"

"She's downstairs, dozing I hope."

"Stay at full flank and I will parallel you."

"Octavio, do you notice any change in their actions? "

"Birdcage, they have maneuvered to my west and are going south losing a little separation. Stand by!"

"Birdcage, they're staying in rifle range, which spooks me. I have my suppressed rifle. I may lose this volley if I don't shoot very soon, now!"

"Octavio, wait one, dodge west again. Birdcage Drone, are you with us?"

"I'm about 150 yards behind them out of sight."

"Octavio is with me on-line. He's going to veer west. Their previous actions indicate they may attack. Octavio, patience, let us handle this so Nerven doesn't get waken sand scared. Roberto has a torpedo in the water. It may be too slow. If they fire anything at Octavio, Vanna, take them out. We'll use the torpedo on the second boiler, be ready to back us up if we miss or don't seriously disable it."

Birdcage Drone, "Standing by."

Octavio, "Veer west, NOW!"

Lance with steel determination to protect the new girl, "Birdcage Drone, there's a tracer at Octavio. End it!"

"Roberto, what's yours doing?"

"They're not firing at Octavio, they're firing at us. I released two torpedoes."

"Too slow!"

"Birdcage Drone, we have sniper fire. Green laze the second boat."

"Roberto, use tracers to keep their heads down while the torpedo tracks."

"Birdcage Drone, if the first boat is sufficiently disabled, cover Roberto and me with the laze now.

"Roger, I've saved your ass before and will gladly do so again."

It takes a Seal to find humor in a firefight.

"Octavio, what's the situation with the first boat?"

"Dam it, Birdcage, I'm still waiting for the torpedo. Ah, excuse me Vanna, and Roberto. It's here. Wait one."

Roberto, "Birdcage, I've been raking them with fire; they keep popping up. "Whack-A-mole". I think Vanna hit only the boiler and they're still functioning."

"Roberto, get down out of line of fire immediately!"

Lance, "Vanna, you got some cleaning up to do!"

"Roger, anything for the step brother-in–law. Out!"

"Roberto here, both laser and torpedo collided at the same time. Only oil on the water."

"Octavio, sitrep?"

'Birdcage, my heart started beating again. There is clean-up; will you handle it for both boats. Nerven is stirring. She doesn't need to see whatever there may be."

"Octavio, understood and agreed. Don't go far. Go out two hundred yards south and circle. I've got you this far, I'm not going to lose you to any anomaly following us."

Lance, "Roberto, take us first to the oil spot."

"Nothing but oil and gas, no implements. It's 400 feet deep here."

"Roberto, flank toward the other boat; drop a flare here."

"Roger."

"Octavio, can you talk down Nerven for five more minutes? There'll be a flare I don't want her to see forcing you to lie."

Up north they do enough lying for the whole world.

"A pleasure. She has dressing moves needing more than five. Circling, Out!"

"Roberto, we need to brick two or three things nobody should see to Davy Jones. When Octavio's bow shoots away, drop another flare."

We caught up with Octavio and escorted him unmolested into the break water at Sambo Creek.

Nerven had the right smile.

"Roberto, I think we hit a raw spot with our jinks to the west. Time for a visit to the north SPS docks."

CHAPTER TWENTY FOUR

Pacho's Evil Sits And Spins

"I stayed and paid. See you sometime, whores!"

Pacho jumped out of the bordello in a decrepit taxi and headed off to TACA's direct flight to Houston. The Rolls took him back to San Antonio. Even a three hour flight demands a whole day. He showered in his Villa, Delores professionally soothed, and he hit the sack.

South-west Don J. Mondo had acted. Pacho selected his garbage scow crews. Nine for trawlers with one on each barge. A rotation having one loading in Texas, one en route south, one sleeping in SPS and finally heading to Texas north-west of Orilla ripping the reef. Within two months, the garbage didn't sink fast enough and the already pollution-challenged Orilla had more ringing the island. Little used pristine reef was choking in excrement. In return, U.S.waste management was in action benefitting corporations with 70% less costs. Re' repression passed the other 30% onto local citizen's taxes. The Senator crowing!

The environment was dying, the corporations flourishing. Nobody knew, or wanted to know their Cartel poster-boy benefactor. He had his purchased pleasure women and wealth in homes throughout tax shelters in the region. Wallowing in his greed, he had another idea. Don J. smiled. Maybe it could take down the Federal Department of Justice, too.

CHAPTER TWENTY FIVE

The Shadow Mission

Laxmi hovered protectively over the start-up of every new Peace Corps. Project. Connie returned every month; it was honeymoon all over. He often visited her on site with every intention of getting out of site. He was a product of the outdoors and grew up on a subsistence farm. He knew every nick and cranny of forests around his clay home in the region. He knew every animal and healing plants. He was a loner by nature and lived happily with the occasional visits. The Gurkha regiment turned everything upside down.

Fifteen years later in retirement, he had found comfort, a woman's devotion, and forests to explore. He could be out for days, but never miss honeymoons. Few others knew him, he was a wraith.

From their nights at A&M, Biblically and personally Alicia Marie knew his core. She was waiting for the right moment to launch him on the trail the Brahmin had plotted with her.

You could find him visiting the Veterinary and helping with the operations. He was drawn to large animals of unique jungle heritage. His options always for horses. If there were a complicated life-threatening injury with a smaller animal, Alicia Maria was quick to consult.

It was on a warm, rainy day Laxmi was sheltering in the clinic while Ceasrito was purchasing supplies in Cuenca. Alicia sat him down for a serious talk. She reviewed the animal's people called the Cartel. He had recognized them long before, in other countries, too, but was quiet. She explained Ceasrito's background and desertion from the local gang. She spoke vaguely of information gained from her father. She spoke of the torture. With tears in her eyes, she recounted her struggle and fear for bringing a child innocent to this desperate pit.

"Laxmi, I need to speak honestly from the start. I met you at A&M and after some memorable love, surprisingly, forgot you. I feel embarrassed about that. When the baby came, I again thought of you. You can enjoy that train of thought. I flew up to see your Brahmin with my fears. We pondered for days. Ultimately, I was sure a man of your character and background was the safest, best answer. It wasn't completely an accident you are here now.

My father has been in the Honduran government previous to the Cartel and still has a few ties. Your friend, Devi, is strongly respected by the U.S. State Department. That government has lost values, ethics, and decency. I checked non-governmental sources. I have a two-year old boy who's going to survive in a very dangerous environment. He is going to face pure evil and will have to go through it here. I can't take Ceasrito to the U.S. and hope to have him considered for any kind of visa. They know who his father was.

There is resentment in right-wing circles here: Ceasrito, and me, as well, should be punished for abandoning their terror gangs. There have been two half-hearted attempts to attack or burn. Ceasrito is good of heart and I love him, but, only my gumption and shrieking caused us to survive, saved us. I am sure you understand where this is going. Please stay with me for two other things. First, Connie's involvement in all this was neither anticipated nor expected. She was a university friend. I have never spoken of this. Your meeting in Nepal was a surprise. Perhaps I had some influence on her transfer to Central America. I'm fooling myself. These things are decided at Devi's level or above.

You and Devi are the only people who know. Ceasrito is innocent and naïve, he could inadvertently destroy me and my boy. One mistake is terminal. The other thing concerns me is were you hurt or emotionally damaged in your wars and couldn't endure any further stress. This is the most hurtful thing I have ever considered. You must protect Connie by not telling her. From Ceasrito's occasional reactions, I know how this coud hurt.

Laxmi, in soothing British tones, "Alicia, I have had free will in arriving here. I had no idea you were here. I was the one who ghosted from A&M. We spoke of Karma. It led me to Connie. It has continued for you with Ceasrito."

I learned much more about you than love, western style. Your intelligence and ability to survive in dangerous surroundings are laudable. I've been in the swilling back rooms, know the emptiness of distorted minds. There is no way to heal the harrowing radicalization tortured into these creatures.

Shiva was our devil and hell in Nepal. The legends of his demonism don't hold a candle to this. I don't relish but realize death will have to be part of this life if I want Connie. I will face every risk."

CHAPTER TWENTY SIX

Nerven Faces The Challenges

Vanna may have had a hint. I was not anticipating the stunning woman Rayban found, and won. She was a couple of shades more bronze than he and his brother. Made hazel eyes glow even brighter. She didn't have ancestry in the North Coast Culture. He had to be a veritable crooner. The other surprise was her being a diver. A connect with Vanna for sure.

You might hear me as the strident leader in a fire fight, but here I was all eyes. Buxom wetsuit required. No wetsuit tonight. I looked. Vanna knew Octavio even medically in depth. Thus, my respect for Nerven didn't get me a boxing of ears. I did have to make a comment about her huge hat.

CHAPTER TWENTY SEVEN

A Deal Breaker?

As the dinner waned, Rayban and Nerven wandered away to visit the Manatee nests. She had enhanced his pride meeting with his friends. He was confident now he could describe the realities of life with him. He told her about the struggle over protecting the Manatees from the Cartel teenagers. She stopped him.

"Honey, you know my dad owns the bar. I didn't know your or that you were involved in these activities. You may not know the exploits of your hidden environmental actions have traveled to bars beyond the Pan Handle. Now I am getting the un-embellished account, I couldn't be more proud of you and to be your fiancé. I should probably be more welcoming to Lance."

"Nerven, true, Good Samaritan Behavior. There are more, seriously dangerous things going on. I fear to tell you. Distraught to lose you, I can't live with myself if something happened to you because I didn't prepare you with the truth. No criticism if you left me right now. I'm certain you will re-evaluate Lance, and Vanna, and Roberto, although you don't know him as well."

"Rayban, I may not have the second ring, but I'm going no place without you. I don't fear. We know each other well, certainly well enough to predict a successful marriage and family."

Nerven continues, "There is more related directly to what we are discussing. I have worked in the bar since I wasn't old enough legally. These cruel chauvinists daily shamed me. Of course, under present circumstances, you, I welcome. They individually get their come-uppances. Every one of them has since, paid a hurtful price. They get viscous responses from me and I don't avoid sensitive parts. Drunk, they walk home; I can strike and leave scars. This is a constant battle. I tone down one uncivil guy via a world of pain, a new thug shows up and I have to start over again. We do have a pistol behind the bar. Dad says use could lose customers who aren't even aware of my injuries. He can mix a debilitating drink. I am very accurate with a pistol or rifle. Am I glad to be here with you where I can be a sexy woman and not be sleeping with painful bruises?"

"I'm sorry you've faced such disgusting behavior", Rayban with venom. I'm glad to have you here where such things are not tolerated even in excited loving. I cannot bare to give any pain in love."

"There are deadlier conflicts here with the cartel, effectively life and death, and much death. This is way beyond bar harassment. I don't relish, but am involved for self-defense and now I depend on the others."

"This Cartel depravity pre-dates me. Protection of my business has put me vulnerable. There is no way this will stop anytime soon. I can't maintain a business without joining the resort owners and the Captain of the Floating Suburb. Can you still, seriously deal with this?"

"I haven't had the life and love you offer, Nerven whispers, nor have I ever anticipated it was close, until you. Risks I will gladly take; outliving this ugly inhumanity with you."

"Fine, let me tell you something positive. Sambo Creek is a close community. I have special relationships because my business brings thousands of dollars to town. We have faced the Cartel occasionally in the past. We unite and protect each other. I can guarantee your safety here in sexy clothes or not. Dealing with the Cartel out on the island or on the water is another thing. I should tell you more."

"Rayban, you can go on telling me grueling stories; at some point "diminishing returns" set in. This problem will go on for a long time? How many years did I have to fight off depraved drunk men? It continues!"

Nerven having had enough, "Finally, the Cartel. I know their ilk. They're often the most disgusting at the bar. Have I not heard the braggadocio of their drink in the fights they supposedly fought? Their recounting of the legend of the Manatee is a hoot. Black phantoms in the night who can't speak. I count the numbers increasing as their fantasy war goes on? Some get so drunk they forget they told the story and repeat it again. Can I not recognize these animals have no direction in their radicalized life other than destruction?"

"Rayban, I ask because I do."

Nerven firmly, "listen one minute more and let this rest. Do you believe I was quietly dozing in the bedroom of your cruiser with radio chatter so intense, rifle fire so obvious, detonations so close, and some flickering of a green ray or something? I wasn't dozing or anything of the kind. I see the love in your eyes, but I am not an innocent unaware woman in a cocoon that you may be imagining. I was tense and praying I'd never hear your pain hit by a projectile. My blood pressure was spiking because I could do nothing to protect you. You tried to calm me in sensitive ways. I was writhing inside with fear for you, and for me without you. I don't want to face such a situation, ever, where I can't actively be involved. It's hard to internalize as nice as your family and friends are, I am here uniquely and only for you. If you are gone, I have nothing. I willingly put all my eggs in your basket and we will have joy. If it ends, I want to go, standing by your side. None of this is a "deal breaker!"

"Rayban, maybe if I am pregnant someday I will relent. In the meantime, face my heart break if you don't depend on me. If you have some specialty military offense or defense to teach me tonight, go on. Otherwise, with your family home and friends on the cruiser, there is a flat area of soft grass inland of the Manatee nest. We belong there!"

CHAPTER TWENTY EIGHT

Job Description

Connie was back from the wilds with bells on, so Alicia Marie stepped back to give Laxmi a chance to whisk her away to some continued honeymoon. She was not certain he could keep such an intense responsibility to himself.

Besides the prime importance of the baby, she spoke of her vow to help merchants fight the Cartel, starting with her friend, Roberto's, tricky shrimp situation.

All eyes were big and wet the next morning. There was disbelief and surprise cloaking them. He asked if they could go out to Southwest Key for a long weekend before she went back to the Moon. My proof of secrecy had held. Connie's eyes would have shied away.

"Better yet, I'll get you a ride."

Octavio, dually manned and womaned swerved into the bay ten minutes later. They were off.

Alicia had tossed the coin and decided to take the risk or never get the "stones" to do it at all. She needed Railroad Juan and his eyes and ears. It could be death to depend on Ceasrito for any of this. Ceasrito knew Laxmi only as a fellow horse aficionado. She pondered if Juan and Laxmi should ever formally meet. Or if she should maintain the task of cross path communication. She decided to keep them apart to start.

CHAPTER TWENTY NINE

Juan And The Railroad Street Regulars: The Team In The Mist

Juan had, over several years, encountered orphaned boys and some little girls, parents executed. In his 20's, he had seen what life had been before the Cartel. He remembered in his adolescence, he'd sworn to do something to stop it. Great plans in adolescence often fall by the wayside. The horrors and extortions he saw built him deliberate. He couldn't do it alone. It required local waifs who knew the reasons, and could dissolve in the night. Most had lost partial or full families. They could never get caught. Most action happened in the misty shadows of the night.

A fireplug of a guy, his five foot five stature didn't cause younger guys or girls to shy away. His knowledge of every alley and path in and around Cuenca amazed his initial group of twelve. They quickly learned to vanish.

Growing trust with his Railroad Street Regulars, his projects were moving from ignored to angrily cussed by the lieutenants. Three years of sniping in the night led to a stark opportunity to join another group fighting the same Cartel.

The Starr Scuba Resort opened and boats went from Cuenca to Guanaja. They were hijacked by the Cartel in front of his very eyes; food supplies and equipment stolen or deep-sixed.

Zulinda, owner of Unclad.com on south Guanaja, met with Lance to develop defense. Juan was known to Zulinda because he had helped build Unclad three years earlier. She brought his name up in their first discussion. They devised a defense and didn't see each other more than once a month thereafter.

Lance spent some time at the American Bar in Cuenca and came to some of the week-end long dances. Indirectly, Zulinda arranged for Juan to meet him. Stand-offish, wary, leery, they got to know each other. Snipped attacks began at this time in the resort's life. On several occasions, Juan got on his sea-based radio and warned Lance of impending attacks. Lance remained shy. Juan warned correctly the third time. Lance headed flank in the security craft to research this guy's bonafides. Obviously he wasn't a Cartel guy. Juan recognized Lance immediately and motioned him to meet in a shadow. Noisy young kids were running around.

After some fencing and testing, Lance said "We need to speak more."

He took Juan down to the bar at the edge of town. It consisted of a dozen empty cable rolls flipped on their side. Self-service was the only service. They had their privacy, except for those same street urchins running around in circles.

Juan expressed his feelings recounting some missions he had completed against the Cartel. Lance burrowed seeking why Juan knew so much of what was going on, or going down before it did. Why could he know and warn the resort?

"Lance, I told you uptown my motivation feels a career. What is bad for the Cartel is my reward. You are facing them with comparatively limited resources. I could be your ally. As for the forewarning information, I don't have someone inside the Cartel so far. That event is clearly doubtful. I do have the Railroad Street Regulars as trained scouts. With the thug's liquor consumption and Regulars' sharp ears, several cross-checked threats find me every night. You have expressed some distress about these boys and girls running around us here tonight. Watch! One whistle."

The sand flipped up footprints and every child ran for Juan's side, warning in their eyes. They formed a circle, a group hard to attack.

With respected stance, Juan quieted them. "No se preoccupe, este hombre es nuestro amigo contra los ladrones. Mano a mano vamos a molestar."

"Ahora, que vaya a su propio bar con orejas abiertas!"

"These kids have assigned bars and know every street and every alley. We have completed some very debilitating action against high level Don J.'s."

Lance replies, "Notable! We don't sign contracts at the resort. Agreements are signified by a handshake. I offer and ask what we owe for the information you've shared? Oh, and Juan, Roberto says Alicia wishes to see you in the next two weeks."

Juan responded, "Ok to Alicia. Lance, we're not some form of mercenaries. We're in this to clean our country. These kids have watched and experienced horrid things done to their friends and families. They have seen what no child should ever see. Their bodies are small; their hearts are scarred. They couldn't be more serious. We have resources to feed and equip all the troop. If I needed more, I'd not have too much pride to ask. For now, your team with shared goals is a worthy asset. Don't underestimate Zulinda as a resource. We need to dissolve now to avoid the Cartel linking us with the Regulars. "

Lance turned and the fireplug was nowhere to be seen.

CHAPTER THIRTY

Eminent Corporate Greed: Collateral Damage

Pacho summarized the inefficiency of the garbage deliveries. He proposed a solution to the Southwestern Don J. The Mondo said, "Great", and beat it from the Villa post haste.

As vile as the Donny J was, he was reluctant to be seen with brain-washed Pacho. His greed was worthy of a position on the defeated outgoing Federal administration; his evil, the idol they followed.

The barges went south with the garbage, dumped it, east towards SPS. Reversed, slept three hours, and peppered the waters with M-80's, firecrackers and small sticks of dynamite to limit explosions back to Orilla. Every living form of life was ripped from the reef and floated to the surface. Fish, octopus, flounder, and squid were netted from the large welded screen into boxes owned by the peons. The less valuable items in a market were left to die on the surface.

Now the corporations didn't want to see Pacho. They lied and let him tear away. He could skim and still pay an additional $1000 per boat to the Mondo for the thug Corps. Located out of SPS, some of the north coast Cartel guys approached Pacho to cash in on a percentage for port fees. Some of the north coast cartel boys were "lost at sea."

CHAPTER THIRTY ONE

The Long Term Proposition

Laxmi and Connie thumbed a ride back with Octavio the following Tuesday. By the look in their eyes, Alicia knew if Connie wasn't on the pill, she'd be five days gone. Woman to woman, she knew she was on.

Heart beating for the next honeymoon, Laxmi waved from the clinic as Connie left to her moon.

Wasting no time, Alicia put ice tea on the wooden picnic table, and hoped he was at least refreshed enough for the long term protection mission.

"Alicia, I didn't discuss this mission with Connie. I did need to know what she thought might be our timeline here. If we're going to be here for a year or two, I couldn't leave your child without protection. Once bonded, my responsibility lives on, according to my culture. A dependable replacement would remain on my mind with occasional, personal monitoring required."

Laxmi continues, "Honduras itself has scores of villages to profit. The Peace Corps head office continues to exist here, and with her international record she takes over the whole region. Maybe a couple of decades. I'd be here for some of the most difficult years you speak of, so I can say "yes".

"Laxmi, I am relieved. The next step is to agree on a contract. This will be a salaried position. For cover you can work along with us as assistant veterinarian, previous experience in Nepal valuable. You live in your house with lunch and dinner together.

According to your senses of the forest, or informants, you decide what your hours should be day and night. Salary remains in force no matter if there are safe times. I know what your Gurkha retirement is. I don't want an argument from you because you are retired; your culture does not permit additional salary. If you have a cultural issue, understand you are here to protect us, and if you didn't have a salary, someone in the government sniffs. The salary will protect me."

With a smile, Laxmi responds, "I guess you're a difficult boss to argue with. I have, however, argued with the Scottish. Don't push me into their mode."

Alicia closes, "Here, we shake hands on these things".

CHAPTER THIRTY TWO

Investigation Begins In Sps

As the U.S. government fell prey, D.J. Mondo, an ideologue with an incomparably stupid grasp of foreign policy, pursued a tantrum of insult toward allies. Before that, there was a drone reconnaissance base near Cuenca. Its call sign was Songbird and the officer in charge had been on the ground and among the people and knew the challenges of the brutal Cartel and running a business in a failed country. We could trust him and timely information.

The D.C. swamp swarmed into a cess pool and DaLJoy of the slimy suit was assigned here, intending to shut it down. Not a word of Spanish. The Re. group now calls the shots. No help offered anywhere, the resort was investigated for protecting the environment. Any communication followed the book and only the antiquated book. For three years, we avoided communication or request for assistance.

On a Monday with Octavio returning Nerven from a fish delivery and family visit, the military-band radio sounded off. Problems for sure. Lieutenant John Clark's voice boomed over." The Force had answered.

"Birdcage, Songbird here, letting friends know I'm back in the neighborhood. My replacement who didn't speak highly of your operation is gone and that we can discuss over dinner. I'm back from Costa Rica. Over and out for now."

Without delay, Nerven and honorary 'Mama' put out a Sunday feast. The "Suit" in tandem with typical present government behavior had been convicted for child sexual molestation, and female trafficking. Those eyes of a lying rejecter of subpoenas won't see a palm tree again. How I hope! (Surely he was a "great guy." I appointed him.) A loyal Re; had scores of photos at Pimp a Largo. He slipped through the cracks and didn't get a pardon.

Having Songbird back as a friendly resource, we invited Rayban, Nerven, Roberto with Cindy, Vanna, and I to the resort to discuss options. We invited Octavio Junior who was a strapping teen-ager now.

Brearly had spooked me with comments about something going on in the west. I was reluctant to even venture into those waters. Comments, vague from Songbird egged me on. I had enough strife going on in and around the Bay islands. Brearly was pleased we were going. A promise the black helicopters would be at ready if we got jumped.

We picked a rainy day in spite of the poorer signaling of the drones. Brearly had his up and Songbird was up very high. Maybe too high. My plan was to focus on what the water in the port might tell. Camouflaged, our boats easily lost in the rain. We took our security boat and a deeply hidden Octavio, canvass draped all over.

We ran hard, four bells for both boats until Vanna warned us off. We backed down to burble speed to enter the hidden marsh. There were enough tall cat-tails with acres of brush. We could see but not easily be seen.

Hidden, we arrived an hour before dawn to deadly quiet. Eyes made radar scans in every direction. I checked Roberto and Vanna in our boat: human radars. Rayban, pegged to Nerven scanned from his cruiser with a smile.

Movement finally. A ragged haired, long dirty black beard stepped out of the square building. He carried a slop bucket and emptied it half way out next to the pier. Fish were flashing away from the area as he hawked his acid reflux onto the water. Our Guanaja boats shared faces of disgust.

Another hour passed. I knew my crews were beginning to savor heading back. I held a stone face. The smoke of what they would be swilling down turned our stomachs. Three joined the line, with the first slop-carrier behind.

In ten minutes, two stumped out to set the twenty footer free from the pier. Shoulder bags dripping white, riding on the edges of the gunwale. Money offered a flaunt of drug laws. Not our prey today.

Three more groups of two detached their twenty footers. One came our way and we ducked. Headed south, he missed us. The other two left using the north wind-break. Heavy exhales, we settled back down, adrenaline dissipating.

The sun grew reflecting off the hills behind the port. It was reducing our stealth. I turned to the electric motor. Vanna moved to pull. Viewing her feminine form, my eyes swept up over the transom. I pointed. Our jaws dropped.

I swerved to Rayban, signing to stop engine ignition. Nerven was in the stairwell. He didn't see me. She did. She catapulted out of the well, pushed his wrist from the throttle; hugged him to the pilot's room floor, turned his eyes to the north entrance. She noted his understanding, and lovingly helped him up.

CHAPTER THIRTY THREE

Protecting Roberto's Shrimp Farm
From Bankruptcy

Roberto and Alicia had been classmates in the K-12 English medium school in Cuenca. They were good friends. He went to Midwest University and she to Texas A&M. Summers, they might see each other at the beach or the best quality restaurant. The friendship endured, but remained platonic. Alicia came home after graduation with a handsome admirer who lived 40 minutes along the north coast. They had been dating at school until she learned his father was the head Don J. of the brutal Cartel on the north coast. Relationship went to stutter-stop.

He was heart-broken and innocent enough not to be aware of his father's involvement. He learned later. She was magnetic in her beauty and top of the class in her intelligence. He was the male mirror image of her beauty. She was controlling and he was complacent and willing. There were few disagreements. She created a resounding 'night with her' and her plan was accepted the next morning.

Now she had the baby; she also had Laxmi as lab assistant and more importantly, as security for the boy from the cartel.

Roberto graduated a year before Alicia. He had bought a shrimp farm and "Swim with the Dolphin" pool on the very south-west Peninsula of Roaban Island. His dad agreed he could have the fancy-free year to travel Europe; fine-tuning his native Spanish with the Spain 'th' in Madrid. He didn't get past Spain; returned alone. He had met Cindy, a Peruvian woman. They had been deep in a relationship in Madrid and around Spain. When he had to go, heartbreaks were physically painful. They struggled on "What's App" and lasted for six months. She flew back to Lima and he met her, her family, married and exported her to Roaban.

They met the others and settled successfully into Dolphins and Shrimp. Successfully until the cartel extorted the restaurants with threats to families, his market. A new Mondo mafia boss decided to take the Dolphin Concession. Roberto with his father sought legal protection. All levels of law enforcement and related government offices were on the Cartel's payroll. He struggled on for a couple of years, but on a moment of weakness, he told Lance and Vanna about his situation. They had been facing the same and sometimes petitioning Roberto for help. Three months later, the Guanaja Island group struck back.

The shrimp business improved for a year and the Cartel struck back again. Alicia had been listening.

Roberto introduced Cindy to Alicia and Cesarito at Jorje's quality restaurant. Brearly was there and introduced his Maria. Alicia Marie learned for the first time what her estranged father in law had done to her old friend, Jorje. She quietly swore to fight back at the right moment with the required resources.

CHAPTER THIRTY FOUR

Ground-Mapping In Sps

Nerven kept Rayban's head down as a Vietnam War era river gun-boat ground in to the dock, and ground as a stinking barge followed. The gunboat reversed and swerved to bring the barge up to its side putting both boat and barge prow-out next to the dock.

Ragged food-sticking beards swarmed from the rectangular building with barrels and boxes soon chained to the barge

I motioned to Vanna and Roberto to look over the gunwale slowly and briefly. Nerven moved Rayban craning over a similar position on his cruiser. Peeking occasionally, we waited for three hours. I heard a hawked cough; a lashed out response of invective. Somebody was sleeping, or trying and bleary drunk. The sun was approaching late morning. After approximately three hours, the commanders emerged shouting the peons into submission to depart. Engines cranking, voices swearing and long handled nets slapped into position. The gunboat growled back north the way it had come, metal reef rippers waiting to desecrate thousands of years of growth.

Three hours noted, this was our cue and we went to full "burble" sneaking around east and north of the breakwater. We succeeded in getting Vanna's signature-mile north. We reached flank-three east to their west; all hell broke loose. Baby blasts forewarned a miniature war. I was listening for a mortar to whistle by. A fire fight right where the gunboat had headed. Suddenly it was, at our distance, completely quiet. I had an idea; the drone to confirm.

CHAPTER THIRTY FIVE

Alicia, Laxmi, Vanna, And Juan Railroad Regulars: Four Against Extortion.

A certain tension existed. Alicia couldn't countenance the direct introduction of Laxmi to Juan. She and Laxmi had scouted the layout of the first restaurant east of the clinic.

Juan Railroad complains, "Alicia, we are on the same team here. Why the secretive voodoo about your other partner?"

"Oh, we do know about him and have since he arrived with Connie. He's a clever forester. We tracked him to Moon village the first time he went with Connie."

Moonlight displayed how sweetly the marriage is proceeding. Nepali, his English accent and movements in the dark confirm a Gurkha. His name is Laxmi and is a loner, polite if addressed.

"You know the skill of our group and we have never failed you."

"Why?"

"Juan, now listen carefully. There is no offense intended. This behavior on my part is not some kind of serendipity. Listen well because of my respect for you and your group. You have saved my whole family on various occasions. I couldn't be more beholden to you. You are part of my ability to do what I am doing."

"The efforts of your large group of Regulars are the only shining lights in this sick society. You, I can't risk. You know the general plans for returning self-choice to owners. You know how complicated and dangerous parts of it will be. Laxmi knows it well. You know what has been going on in the night from his protective processes. You know it better than me. You have protected me in the night and showed you are effective. I have Laxmi here for several reasons. I try to avoid ever putting him in the same place with you. For the safety of your group, you need to avoid him. The decent people can't afford to lose your support if you are ever caught linked to him. I will continue to be the go-between avoiding the worst. I hope you can accept it and stay with me. I will never insert myself between you and your Regulars. Independently, please continue to do the helpful things you do so well."

Alicia continues, "We did reconnoiter the first restaurant last night. These people have had their families threatened so will be more than skittish. Using whatever respect I have as a known veterinary, I will quietly begin by meeting with them. I will start tonight. Both you and Laxmi can be in the environs although I expect no push back in the short run. I will occasionally give a progress report to Roberto but don't want him anywhere around. No discussion with Cesarito. The restaurant tonight is in the trees. If I can be convincing, it will be a good place to start."

CHAPTER THIRTY SIX

No Loose Ends

Away from the explosions, returning from the SPS observations, I contacted Brearly saying, "Up-date in the morning."

He expressed relief we were all ok. I had expected him to be more exuberant.

I wasted no time in getting the drone up to validate my predictions. I waited an hour to see the gunboat leave the gutted Orilla area south of the island heading north-east. The water around the boat was littered with the colored wrappings of M-80 fire bombs, short sticks of dynamite, and a field of dying reef life. The north-east tack took it south of Orilla to avoid the garbage ripper coming south from Texas.

Rogue lights glimmered constantly when Octavio got north and west of Roaban. He was no farther north nor west than the windward tail of the floating suburb.

CHAPTER THIRTY SEVEN

Heartbreak And Frustration

Maria and her Weatherby escorted us well before wind interference. She was unusually quiet. Brearly was morose in his big captain's chair. We were excited to report but settled down sensing dismay.

He said, "Go ahead, Vanna first."

I finished with the distant explosions off Orilla to our stern.

He thought forever; weakly thanked us for putting together the final pieces of the puzzle. His demeanor sickly with loss of self-confidence. This was way out of his parameters. I confronted him about his attitude and particularly his health. If it's serious and we are involved, we need to know.

"Lance, I need a nap now."

Maria escorted us back to a much anticipated interlude and a prelude in the bubble. The extreme stress and danger left Vanna in rivulets of relief. We could make no sense, so we de-stressed, wrapped up and napped.

Brearly rebuffed business until all was eaten with the Maria': "cherries jubilee". The chromosomes were surely from a French conquistador. It was obvious she knew his delicacies and the cherries were especially for him.

He took two generous shooters of Southern Comfort. We had never seen such behavior from him. We couldn't relax. How bad could this be?

"Lance, Vanna, this began to be obvious the trip before Octavio brought Nerven. It had been in operation. If we hadn't had the D.C. swamp slime in Songbird, we'd have known long before. The western movements of Octavio stirred a bee's nest on the shorelines between the Island Suburb and Orilla."

Brearly got the hint; launched Black Bird to the southern coast of Texas. Returning, a slow monitor skirting Orilla, opened the evil box. The disdain, greed and corruption immediately bare, sickly exposed.

I didn't say anything to you because I heard rumors the U.S. government or its self-appointed congressmen were involved. You are much more exposed than our Floating Suburb. These owners can fight the outgoing filth dollar for corrupt dollar.

Brearly continued, "They had some crook named Pacho Mountanya, Cartel trained, corporation and Re-funded, and directing corruption for large corporations near the damaging storms. He started out transporting garbage from the affected companies to an area southwest of Orilla. He decided since his barges were returning empty, to dynamite the reefs and scoop whatever came to the top. On return, he delivered to wholesale dealers in the bayous. The conspiracy between him and the corporations along with seed money from the Cartel made him rich."

Brearly continued, "I learned the whole story, I went to the authorities in Texas. I received the same response you got from the cartel front in Tegucigalpa. I was shocked the cartel had gotten enmeshed with U.S. authorities. I went higher and got nowhere. I went to once trusted fellow military officers and got nothing. I was near to tears. There was no law, nor enforcement under this train wreck corrupt government. I was broken. I returned to Maria who nursed and encouraged me in another attempt to protect."

"I tried hiring mercenaries with catamaran boats to harass or even sink the war vessels. Gunships blew them out of the water. I met with our corporation board and they permitted use of the black helicopters. They had enough success the routes to the bayous got too dangerous to be profitable. We focused on the Texas garbage trade. On our second attack, two fighter jets strafed our helicopters. What cartel girl is in bed with a U.S. Air Force major? Whoever, he had a role-model leader right at the top."

We reset and concentrated on short attacks from protected copter bases. We could be out and back before the jets could get there. It was a fight of a mouse with an elephant. We began to feel some success. The following morning, six fighter/bombers emasculated all our bases.

Maria entered, "Brearly wasn't injured, but came home in tears. His pride in the government he had fought for, was broken."

Brearly, "And dammit, I see no way to stop this. It will affect us and surely your diving."

Vanna shifted, "I have some ideas you might consider. Let Lance and I kick this around."

CHAPTER THIRTY EIGHT

Extortion: Cleansing In Baby Steps

Alicia talked, encouraged, and calmed frightened restaurant owners. It took several weeks to get a man with no family to risk the new push-back.

The Cartel trawler approached the dock in front of the restaurant. The owner came to the dock. I was hidden in the trees. The owner, Pedro, refused the delivery.

"Pedro my friend, you better get your attitude adjusted or you will be selling whatever you may salvage from a horse cart. We'll give you one night to reconsider. Any spoiled shrimp will be on your bill."

They left; I stepped out. "Pedro, you were brave in your response. As I promised, I will take it from here. Get a good night's sleep tonight. You may be disturbed for a few minutes tomorrow night."

"Alicia, I won't be sleeping at all for a while. I'm risking my business on your honesty and strength of character."

"I'm not the only resource you are depending on. I'll stop by if there are any revisions to our plan. You can trust in some noise, mostly a full night's sleep."

CHAPTER THIRTY NINE

Potential Final Heartbreak

After delivery by Maria, walking up the resort path, Lance deftly headed Vanna off, "Blearly may not be lucid enough to read you. I know what you seals would do in this instance. I know exactly what you are thinking. And my heart is in my mouth. We have never put you or ourselves in such danger. I'm torn. Is the Western Caribbean worth the risk you will take? If the worst happens, how will I weigh this against living alone for the rest of my life?"

"Lance, we've made no commitment. The tension was thick over there I couldn't analyze an option to a logical outcome. It's critical to do, and have your devil's advocacy for my safety. You may need to come with me. I think we need to get some unofficial commitment from Songbird. Blearly will surely be with us. There is much more I haven't even touched on in my thoughts."

"It's already too much for today. Let's take a quick shower."

Our quick shower never was nor ever will be "quick". The intensity of our vulnerability to each other and these killers rang in my mind. I know Vanna as deeply as a man can know a woman and she was stone tense. I'm now at a mental stress point.

I stepped behind her as she reached down for the shampoo. I raised her and feinted. She eased back turning only her neck to look into my eyes. Firing, she fixed me and didn't relax. I was destroyed as never before.

"Lance, look at us, right this instant. You have raised me off the floor as though I was light as a regulator. I can lift you only through adrenalin charged great stress. Women always want to say they are as strong as any man. I am strong but not stupid. As this unfolds in my mind, I can see I will need your stature as well as your mind."

"Vanna, you know…….."

"Lance, yes, I know, and I trust. Now, I only need to trust your nature. Call it healing, or mental first aide. Call it anything, but I can't talk or think or wait anymore. Come on!"

I held her tight while she fought off the demons and I fought for endurance. She was afraid more than I had ever seen. I tried to repress, losing in the end. Her stress grew and fear washed off her, mauling me trying to get her relief through some diffusion from my skin. I forced myself to give what she really needed until too tired to be tense.

Weakly she whispered, "Lance, if ever there is a time we should do this together, it is now. I need your warmth."

I released the endurance fight; pressed her at her cliffs, and energized her with romantic friction. The warmth arrived; she was asleep.

CHAPTER FORTY

Pacho Hangs On

With the loss of the helicopters, he could ramp up the garbage end of the transport shutting down the Mississippi routes. There was some reduction of graft monies from the Re. Corporations. He simply reduced commissions to various outliers working indirectly. There was an auditor with the Cartel who quickly noted the reduction of money to the evil coffers of greed.

He soon got a visit at Alamo heights. Donny J Mondo was the Mafioso this time to question. A great choice, he had never run a successful corporation in his life. Look at his bankruptcies. Look at his personal greed. The absolute stellar choice.

The discussion uncomfortably bounced around the costs versus the number of villas Pacho was supporting and country club memberships he was providing. Donny J suggested while profits were down, he reduce some of this lobbying. Pride immaculate in itself, Pacho countered with wild dreams of bombing in the Pacific and bringing the catch into the Caribbean for wholesale. The repartee nonexistent, phrases stuttered, awkward responses.

Finally, Donny, frustrated, said, "Ok, try your ideas. The bottom line is net profit. Deaths be damned!" I urge you to off-load all the villas west of Roaban.

Pacho's final response, selling iceboxes to Eskimos, "No, no. I don't need to lose Deloris. The Pacific will cover us.

CHAPTER FORTY ONE

Shifting Temperment Of Extortion

This was the first attempt to drive shrimp suppliers from Cartel back to Roberto. Alicia knew this could be a do or die. She spoke individually to Laxmi and Juan Railroad, reviewing the odds and in Juan's case, requesting more boots on the ground. Other shop owners were watching like hawks.

CHAPTER FORTY TWO

Octavio's Struggle

A college sophomore, Octavio Junior was going to be the first ever of the family to graduate with a university degree. The family and even the community looked at him as a bubble floating over the fields, fearing something sharp fly by and pop it. Rayban with record of several years of intense efforts, and successes could easily be mayor of Sambo Creek.

Once offered, "Sure, you want me to be a politician. Look to the North to see what a Politician who is not a statesman can destroy. If I'm doing well here, my self-esteem from you couldn't make me prouder. It's time to concentrate on Octavio Junior."

Junior came home two summers and stayed for extra curriculum credits for two. He felt the need to help his father, who was paying ultra-tuition. Rayban would have none of it. To smooth the waters, he let him join with Nerven for a group of three. He also monitored the absolute safest routes. He loved to have him home, was relieved the day he had to return for classes in the slightly safer, but still racist U.S. He could afford to send him to Europe or even New Zealand. Despite the atrocious behavior of the right wingers, up to the moment the U.S. program was strong and flexible opening more paths to graduate studies. Two more years could signal the collapse of that U.S. Curriculum. He would have his diploma by then.

With the concentrated activity around Orilla, there was less pressure on Octavio's trips to Gulfport. Unfortunately, the smaller boats had enough radicalized animals to mount occasional dangerous forays.

Octavio analyzed and decided the Wednesday trip should draw least attention. He and Nerven welcomed Octavio Jr. aboard at sunrise. Being abundantly cautious, he contacted Birdcage for notice of any blockage. At the moment there were none. He pushed off and ran at three bells. Conditions permitting, increase to four passing Guanaja.

Passing the island, he got a demanding notice that a fast Cartel boat was launching from Roberto's shrimp operations pier.

Lance barked, "Octavio, reduce your speed. There is trouble and I need time to re-boot. Steer east north-east at two, no three bells. Maybe if you are moving away, they'll break off. They are streaming some tug block with a few less knots than my Chevy. They may explode. Hold on, check your sea radar, I see a smaller diesel way behind in their wake. I'm pushing off."

"Josh, can you man the drone tower for a while."

"Glad to, this excel program is crossing my eyes. What do you need?"

"Josh, I have never ordered you into a firefight such as this. You listen carefully and do whatever Vanna or I command. If the worst should happen to us, you automatically green-ray decimate all Cartel boats and crews, save Octavio and wait for anything from him."

"Octavio, I know Junior is with you. Everything I use will have him in mind. If you think I am missing a viewpoint you see, do whatever is best for him."

"Vanna, there is something off about this attack. There's some player we're missing. Contact Juan and see if he can fill in the blanks."

"I will contact Juan, remember, he is supporting the "extortion reduction" mission."

Lance resets, "Dicy, if Juan is tied up, tell Roberto to fast track up here. Give him our location. Contact Songbird and see what he can offer."

Vanna quietly adds, "Roger, Remember who wants to live with you forever and make your decisions accordingly."

"Roger, out, sweetheart."

Blackbird growls onto the radio. "Birdcage, go to camp radio. No other ears need hear. You're trying to analyze what's different here from other attacks. I believe I know. I respect your character and success, I need to call this one."

"Excuse me, Songbird here. Do you read?"

"Five by five, Songbird. Blackbird, we can discuss my involvement. Please shut down for a minute. I have something coming in from Songbird."

"I'll stand bye but this is not a happy camper over here. From me, come your helicopters. Out!"

"Back to you Songbird, what have you got?"

"Birdcage, you and Octavio are being pursued by a big discontinued block shaped boat. Narrow bow, a barge. Further away there is a smaller diesel which I don't think will play any roll."

"Roger, I have those on radar."

"Birdcage, I know you're concerned about the barge. It's big, its optics emerge faster to you. You and Octavio are pulling away in good measure. I think I know the slime pilot there. I urge you not to engage him in the present area. You are heading to Gulfport harbor, correct?"

"Yes".

"Focus on that, forget about the lumbering barge; get in the harbor of the breakwater. He will break off. Songbird, Out!"

Lance relays, "Octavio, did you follow?"

"Roger, I wish I trusted the U.S. government like I used to, even Songbird, when my boy's and partner's lives are involved. Over."

"Understood, I also have non-governmental information coming from Blackbird who is fuming waiting for me to get back to him. Listen with me on camp radio. Let your crew listen too."

"Birdcage back, apologies. I think I have other information for you. Octavio is on-line."

Blearly frustrated retorts, "Off, finally. Bottom line, Cage, I not only want, but demand to lead against this motley bunch! I know of the garbage crook, and he is on your tail right now. I know you are soon for Gulfport. I will call and you will not get into any fight which you might even win up there."

"Blackbird, help me direct personal care for my close allies by being more specific."

Blearly pants with disgust, "This little dong whose mouth wouldn't digest pig shit was personally responsible for the downing of three helicopters and the lives of four men. Additionally, Greenpeace lost a woman. Collateral damage to humans and reef in the Caribbean goes on and on. My mental attitude toward the country I once served is washed up. Enough?"

Lance softens, "I'm sorry. You do outrank anybody in the trenches here. I'll tell them to follow your lead."

"Thank you. Now, no engagement before or during your time in Gulfport. We will be there a few days. There are other anti-Cartel projects going on which if planned carefully can jointly bring results. Octavio, slow down and transfer Nerven to Birdcage and keep Octavio Jr."

"Black bird, out!"

Lance follows, "Pull your boats together, and avoid using a

radio. The four of you go to ground immediately. You have to hide or camouflage the boats. Nerven, since you grew up there, you may have some options?"

"Yes, I know the port area because my Dad's bar is there. Do you want to discuss these now, or let us do it shortly before we get there?"

"The only thing I know about the city is the entertainment I partook of before Maria. If it's still there, it'd be dangerous. This thug would be there. Avoid."

"Go ahead at your own discretion. Get back up to speed to increase separation with the goons. Black Bird, Over and Out!"

CHAPTER FORTY THREE

Gone To Ground In Gulfport

Nerven quickly responds, "Using what I know, you can fine-tune. I'm a diver, not seasoned. Between my Dad's bar and the seafront is a huge warehouse. It's used to store boats in the winter. It's empty by now. Upon arrival, Octavio and Junior alone go to deliver the fish. We'll quietly move the Chevy up to the door, and hold. When Octavio and Junior finish, we open the door, once, and move the boats in, prow out. We need to organize a canvass or suitcase to carry things we will need in a hotel. With separation, we will go up, staying behind displays, and exit the bar. I'll tell my Dad so he doesn't jump me for joy as though Rayban isn't doing enough."

"There is a B&B owned by a work-friend of my mother. I'll call from the boat here to be sure there are three rooms. While there, we will go out individually, not as a group until we depart. Returning through the bar concerns me. The thug could well be there. Comments?"

Lance looks at Vanna, "Any thoughts?"

She ponders, "I think we'll have to order in food, not to be out in restaurants for any extended time. I share your concern about the bar. We should take re-breathers from the boat here in emergency. We need to close radios to only specific times we hear from the Captain."

Vanna continues, "I think we have to put duct tape on all running and emergency lights. Junior, we need you to do this after we are moored inside. Find an entrance to the water and go under the planks inside. One of us will monitor from the distance. Nerven pops in, "There was a ramp next to the bar."

Vanna back, "Check as a possible entrance for you and exit for all of us as we depart. Nerven, you could even call and ask your Dad to close the curtains for a few days."

CHAPTER FORTY FOUR

Junior Steps Up

Wearing the wet suit and some burned cork on his mother's bequeathed bronze skin, Junior crept down the street to the ramp adjacent to the bar. From a place you never consider, "Commercial Loving" his Dad watched his every move. He noted the bar curtains were closed and relaxed. Junior slid smoothly into the water. He inhaled not exhaling through the breather until two meters under the surface. Now Dad had to wait.

With only the dim blue light from his cell phone, fish and jellyfish swarmed and wrapped around him causing his movements to be awkward. A stone fish threatened and a squid exploded to the darkness. He jumped over the stone fish and reached the bottom of the sliding ladder. A deep breath. Paused, he realized the fish didn't make him awkward. He was frightened and shivering. He moved under the ladder without raising it and was next to the Octavio with the running lights automatically on. For the moment he could see shadows. He climbed the short ladder firmly and grabbed the duct tape left in place for him.

To get this over as soon as possible, he raced to tape all lenses. He finished the Octavio and couldn't be patient enough to walk up and down the ladders to the Chevy. He leaped ahead to the Chevy, water resisted, he missed every step and hung on the outboard wrenching his shoulder in attempt to avoid a splash. He soon let go and floated to the cement floor. It took several breaths to get him back upright. In pain he reached over to the Chevy ladder and acted appropriately this time. As a now disabled person, he gently worked his left arm to cover the lenses.

Now only his cell was glowing as he ducked to the door. He moved tenderly under and came out noticing how much light was reflecting from the bar. Reminded to avoid making waves, he took a breath and held it till he was well below the surface. Surprising how much noise was escaping from the bar. He knew his Dad would be analyzing his every wiggle. He maintained silent, consistent movement every water-impeded step of the way. Now on the silent traipse to the B&B., he had to pretend he didn't have a pulled muscle.

Vanna met him at the door and helped him out of the wetsuit. Seeing his grimace, she gently massaged his shoulder as he moved toward the shower. The big question mark glowed on her face.

"Please don't tell him about this?"

"Please don't tell him about what?"

CHAPTER FORTY FIVE

Collateral Damage Of The Third Kind

Pacho was not street stupid; pure evil and dumb. The day after Donny J. West left, he packed. He knew what "damaged baggage" gains in a Cartel departure. He left Delores with an uncomfortable red booty and stormed out the door. He could be home free, or at least in Honduras, in a day. He headed for the dock where the barge was loading.

Deloris called two of her girlfriends and gutted the house. Bye slime!

CHAPTER FORTY SIX

The Way Down, Kicking And Screaming, Result; Quiet

He was still the owner; the gunboat command accepted he be left in his own room with meals delivered. When the gunboat reversed mooring and the dynamite was loaded, the dock was still. He dissipated into the woods of SPS. From a duck blind of branches, Juan Railroad watched him go. Now, Brearly knew he was near.

CHAPTER FORTY SEVEN

New Pickings

They knew he was Cartel; not much more. With silver tongue he worked to ingratiate himself with the leadership. Don J. again. No matter how many Don J.s you kill, another "Capo" loyalist rises from the swamp.

He waited for another assignment and waited and waited. Finally, he groused so all could hear. Don J. called him to his office. "And now, what the hell is your problem?"

"I am trained years beyond any of these gooks. I ran a multi-million dollar mission in the Western Caribbean. I'm sitting here twiddling my thumbs. What?"

Mr Mantanya, you ran a multi-million dollar project into the ground. You were cautioned and warned. You knew you were running down here where you thought we wouldn't know of you. I gave you a second chance and a big boat and sent you to interdict the Guanaja group. You lost them in Gulfport and wasted time until I called you back. What the hell else could you screw up?

CHAPTER FORTY EIGHT

Brearly Shares Command

At the exact programmed moment, Black Bird crackled through. "Are you all well?"

Lance responded for the group. "What's up?"

"Can you leave Gulfport unnoticed?"

"We'll leave partially under water."

"Ok, the crook is still in Gulfport. You must be pristine prepared to leave in the early hours, two-thirty recommended. Get out of the harbor on electric motor. At one mile off, squeeze every horsepower your beasts can deliver. You'll be able to take twenty minutes to get necessities at Starr. At high speed run over inside the Floating Island's boat storage. Get everything out of sight. We can plan further."

Three nights ago, Octavio Junior had stealthily slipped down the ramp and taped the lights. His elbow is now healing. Rayban had watched everything in the seedy neighborhood looking for potential dangers. Nothing. The group decided to use the same escape.

Well after midnight they set out with a spring in their step glad to get out of the cooped up B&B. Two widths of hedges and a copse of old trees were left to maneuver to get to the side of the bar. They managed quietly the first. Rayban pushed his head out the second, and "What the hell?" he ducked back again.

"The whole bar is outside wading, splashing water on the ramp."

Vanna edged forward, focusing and retreating. "They are having a freaking wet t-shirt party in the middle of the night over under and around the ramp. The only way we'll get through there is if Nerven and I take it all off. Now what?"

Lance follows, "We have to go tonight. No option. There is no way a white nude and a bronze nude are going to go unseen. We'll have to go back to the unloading ramp and make our way underwater. You have your rebreathers."

Moving back two shrub densities, they trekked the fifty yards to maneuver under water. Junior familiarized them with underwater fauna they need to avoid.

They slipped down the fishy smelling ramp easing themselves into the water. The local girl, Nerven led the group forward. She shooed off two barracuda drawn by Vanna's white skin. She dovetailed and turned creating a path devoid of 'man of wars", bone fish and red fire coral. The docks looming above, Lance slipped up, hit his head and came down shaking the blow off.

Everybody got the message and the rest of the trip re-learned to exhale the breather. It had taken forty minutes to cover fifty yards. They carefully eased their heads out of the water catching each other's eyes. Absolutely still, not a wave.

Frustrated, Junior whispered, "I guess all the girls are wet to full exposure and went inside."

Rayban's face was smiling with chauvinistic pride. He had few chances to see what his young man was thinking.

Lance reset the group. "Things have changed a bit; we can revise. We need to open the door, but not wait to close it. Junior, get on the front deck and reach over, get a grip and open it quickly. Don't worry about noise. The rest of you, start your electric propellers; you hear the door, fire out, not on top of each other. Head directly south to Guanaja. You get one mile out, light off four bell horsepower and keep your heads down to avoid drag."

Josh had stayed up late. Brearly, now comfortable again in command, had him on drone night scope shadowing the group. When they hit the full mile, Josh painted them with the drone radar. There was no other shipping in the channel. He didn't want to tip an enemy off. He didn't radio.

It took two and a half hours at 4 bells before they pulled against their Guanaja dock. Everyone scrambled to get needed belongings for an unknown amount of time. The Suburb would provide meals, Maria in her element.

Once again in their fast boats, they flew under the covered docks of the 'Island.'

CHAPTER FORTY NINE

Shrimp Product Denied

The restaurateurs maintained hopeful patience. The first rejection of product had caused a virulent mouthful of filth. Threats, warnings, vile you have never heard before. Vocabulary training in the putrid ditches had been limited.

One night later, it descended. Two heavily armed thugs went through the woods above the restaurant. They vanished never to be seen again.

Alicia took one careful step further. Seeing the success, the next owner agreed to cooperate with her. She in the trees and the owner facing some danger on the dock, product was rejected. Vitriol again spread.

A day and night passed with no confrontations. Unsettling.

The second morning, Juan reassembled in her operating room and said five were coming on the next raid. "Should we back-up Laxmi?"

"The right idea, I need to get his idea. Are they coming through the trees again? Could you come over again this afternoon, around four?"

"Ok. I don't have confirmed times. There'll be light for a couple hours after four. They'll wait till dark. You are calling the shots to this point, Alicia."

"Juan, thank you for your patience. Protective mothers are obviously difficult to deal with. Have you any idea why they didn't hit us right back last night, as before?"

Juan responds, "I've seen some things to which I can't give context. There may be some new fighter, or leader they're grooming. I'll let you know when I do."

He left back to Cuenca.

Laxmi emerged as a phantom of the windbreak.

Alicia warns, "Laxmi, I have intel the response will be tonight through the trees again with five cut-throats. I can get some back-up if you wish. Wouldn't it make sense with five to one?"

"With extra planks, prepare your burial boat."

CHAPTER FIFTY

One After The Other

Lance and Vanna were rested, on the same track, smoothly breathing, and blush fading when Maria picked them up with her big gun.

Post haste, Maria escorted them up to the dining room behind the pilot house. She quickly put out some breakfast snacks as Brearly settled into his command seat.

We had decided Vanna should start because she had developed a very close relationship. Where he might rebuff me, he would never her. From our many previous experiences together, you might anticipate a jealousy issue here. Not a hint.

Vanna jumped right in. She spoke of our reconnaissance about the boats and barges….. and he stopped her right there.

"I don't mean to be rude. I'm sure you've got this planned beyond my ken. I mentioned on the boat there's another mission on-going. A major battle to provide continuing health to Roberto's shrimp farm. He's already lost the dolphins and only a joint push-back will keep him in business. In the long run it still may not be enough. We have you and your staff and your contact on the railroad, probably the largest and most prepared we could be. It's basically now or never and hope for the long run. First, we connect you with Alicia, the Vet. I think she healed your dog a couple of times. It's a complicated, even dangerous story. Better you hear it directly from her. She's an old friend of Roberto, who, as you would expect, is aware of what's going on."

"No-one must be aware of your meeting." Brearly finishes.

Lance adds, "We'll get Juan to connect us with Alicia. Soon without delay, we need to start on the damage to the reefs and overflow of garbage the sea can't absorb."

Brearly, "Get the shrimp farm out of danger. Finally go ahead with your reef project. I doubt you need anything from me."

Vanna quickly reacts, stress between her eyes, "Captain, you need to hear the plan because you're a critical player."

"Fine, get back to me later."

CHAPTER FIFTY ONE

Miniscule Evils' Demise, Prepared Collateral Damage

"Vanna, Octavio has closer relations with Juan Railroad. We'll go camp radio and see if he can get a meet; his boat a good locale for privacy. Alicia will determine how she will attend. Both Brearly and Roberto trust her. I guess we can. I need to hear a whole lot more detail before I put us in harm's way."

It was a week and a half before Octavio could get all the players together. We met on his cruiser behind South West Key. The meeting lasted the night and Vanna and I learned of another player from Nepal. I was amazed at the risk Alicia had been taking, first to protect her child, then to right Cartel wrongs and hurt them secretly as we did. She surely had a big set of "intestinal fortitude." Cesarito was never involved in any of these actions. There was concern about his naivety getting everybody killed. She was sending him, under duress to continuing horrid cartel pow-wows where he inadvertently gathered useful information. She never let on how his information was used. "Just to protect our little boy." Alicia had many other plans . I was amazed and firmly in her camp by the end of the evening.

We set up communication channels between Alicia, Octavio, and Juan-Railroad. Alicia privately planned with Laxmi.

Something in the wind, Juan knew first. Ceasrito would accidentally say something helpful with no idea of the total puzzle. Laxmi through Alicia was very insightful of danger, guiding in strategy.

Alicia had now drowned thugs out of two restaurants where the cartel had threatened families. The number of cartel responding to their rebuff was growing. Five thugs had come to the second skirmish. No sign in the woods except the tracks of the bodies being dragged to the funeral boat.

Seeing Alicia's promises kept, other restaurateurs agreed to take the risk. Alicia hidden, the owners would meet boats at the dock and refuse their product. Roberto's wholesale market was slowly improving, Risk meandered in the mists. Extortion was hard to kill.

Alicia in the trees, Ricardo, owner of a leading restaurant, faced off with a fourth crass boat of pirates. Same refusal, same vitriol. Two days to mount the punishing attack. Juan immediately called us on Guanaja and Rayban on Octavio. In the darkest of night, Octavio picked us up, quiet running engines. We unloaded our people and our armory downwind of the anticipated attack. Juan kept to the woods, informing us there was a big square barge-boat loading thugs. Three of us set up in locations where we wouldn't get caught in our own cross fire. General Alicia was hunkered down in logs where she could dispatch a few from behind. I didn't see a Nepali, nor did I ever.

In the square boat's pilot house was the renowned Nicaraguan poster boy of the cartel. At the time we were unaware of Pacho's falling out with the cartel. He was trying to regain his stripes. His eyes were black hate; an American-made automatic with an over-the-shoulder ammunition vest. A gift from Texas Oil.

Yellow on the inside as the leadership of these blood-loving animals were, he waited to dismount until many of the others entered the melee. He leaped to the ground and dived over to take Rayban with a scuba knife. Rayban fought him off. Now confident, Pacho pulled his automatic to get distance to raise it and down him. We were all fighting two or more marauders. I looked over feeling sick at what was developing for my dear friend. Our general Alicia didn't have a sight line to the poster-boy scum. I was fighting for my life, trying to disengage, and the FORCE was with us. Vanna's double tap I had learned to love hit his neck; a curved knife landed dividing his lungs. I looked around and saw Vanna, but no one with a knife. Octavio could thank the phantom. She saw where I had lost advantage. Swinging back from saving Octavio and piercing Pacho to his last rest, she glanced behind me; another signature-double.

Scuffles continued with three of Juan's teenage Regulars. My rifle locked but Vanna backed me up. Thugs disappeared, Railroad Regulars In shock.

Octavio, at 6'5" was knife to knife. Brains empty as chaff, they fell off him, ripe walnuts in a north wind. As a herd, they saw the fate of Pacho and jumped to the barge. Others headed up to the woods; came out prone. I scanned the battlefield. The curved knife gone, Pacho's body slithered to the ground.

We helped fill the funeral cruise, then got aboard Octavio and headed back to Guanaja. There had to be ten dead, five not being permitted to heal and attack again, and five on their barge, running, collapsing as Vanna was following the protocol of no survivors. Their barge finally went out of control and slammed an empty dock exploding the illegal armaments bringing ugly flares to the night.

In the meantime: the other owners followed suit and merchandizing returned to fair. New "animals" hatched from rotten eggs and were brainwashed rapidly. Alicia had to have some plan. I certainly didn't!

We had claimed territory back from criminals. For a long time, Laxmi held and appreciation began among the owners. Vanna and I were asked twice more when Juan Railroad predicted something bigger. Life of never being able to let down and relax, except in Germany, was wearing on us.

CHAPTER FIFTY TWO

A Possible Survival Future

Privately, after years of strife, in our bubble our thoughts were beginning to wander to an island in the Adriatic. Rab sat off the new, wealthy country of Croatia, created from the break-up of Yugoslavia. Approximately thirty miles in diameter, I had dived there alone twenty years before. There were four dive resorts equidistant from each other. An ad for a resort for sale crossed our joint worldwide scuba website.

We moved the boats and equipment back to the resort from Brearly's basement. After going to ground in Gulfport and the fire fight for the sea food restaurants right on top of each other, we wrapped up and slept. We lustily re-connected the next day, but the bubble now included thoughts of a long range future. The boat captains had not been involved in either skirmish. We lolled around in the bungalow and kitchen for another day.

As battle after skirmish dragged on, we became more impatient in our bubble. In general things were not going well. Alicia's rebellion against the cartel, even with the power of Laxmi, was waning. The thugs on Roaban constantly feinting attack on the wired fence. Unclad. Com and Starr resort were fighting battles at night keeping guests unaware and unharmed. The odds were turning against us. Brearly was supporting us. His island was impregnable; the only good news.

The constant U.S. government minions allying themselves with murdering Cartels for illegal campaign funds had empowered them into running battles against all of us. Sick empowerment from the top affects unknown millions of people, national and international, directly and indirectly. Voters need to check carefully. Re is the dangerous choice.

CHAPTER FIFTY THREE

Northerner

The weather had been shiftless. The East Troy group got out early morning before the wind. We had had another night chord from the thug congregation but they didn't get close enough for us to take them out. It was another damper on the joy of running the fine Starr resort. For other loads of ignorance the thugs sported, they knew the weather.

I hurriedly slid the drone into the shed with the attached guy poles and cables. I disconnected the electric line trip wires and secured the CCTV. Down on the dock both captains knew the weather and were frantically re-cabling and moving the ramp boats away from the normal dock-side hook-ups. They moved out to connect them with thick titanium cable to tons of ballast off-loaded by a tanker years ago on the verge of leakage and sinking. The three captains were wearing orange life vests planning to swim from the new anchor site back to the dock. The wind was thundering. There was no way. Vanna saw them while trying to get the security boat to a vertical angle up on the beach. She gunned the engine in reverse and threaded the boat through the new cables to pick them up. The waves were tossing them as they helped each other with vice-burly wrists onto the slippery gunwale. Vanna backed the security boat off and ran it right up onto the sand beach. Only the inboard's propellers were left out over the water. The captains sprinted east where their families were hunkering down in bungalows set back in the forest.

Vanna came running up the hill giving me a high five as she

went around the north side of the bungalow tightening the lag bolts as she went. I met her at the East end and we anchored the center pole to a weathered pine. It had weathered eons of Northerner's.

Flying into the door, we flopped down winded as crackling and whining took over the sea band radio. It was Octavio on his cruiser running hard for the airport island for Guanaja.

He had two fat-cat wealthy fisherman. Even with all his stabilizers, two hours back to Sambo Creek was not an option. He was yelling on the radio to Pedro Jet warming up to enjoy the strong wind, a boon to him for take-off from rough Guanaja runway.

Octavio hollered, "Pedro, I have two customers who are doubting their swimming abilities. Let me pull up to the dock and get them and their tackle onto the plane. Get them to a hotel in Cuenca for tonight. I'll take care of them in the morning or when this Northerner clears off."

The wind whipped the client's long pea coats teetering them off the fall to shallow rocky water. A heart attack could this be. Octavio with rippling arms stood them straight to attention; escorting them the rest of the way. They ran to the plane.

Pedro shouted over the wind, "Roger, Octavio, I'll send you the bill for dinner and drinks at Janet's."

"Accepted. I owe you at least one. Now Go!"

As Octavio re-boarded his cruiser, Vanna radioed to see he was ok. He was only 100 yards from the edge of our resort. She said he shouldn't try to run back to Sambo tonight. He could bunk in one of our now empty bungalows.

Octavio, relaxing with a smile in his voice, responded, "Thank you very much guys. I see a light on at Zulinda's. Soft mattresses for sure over there but this time I will be true to Zeren. Out!"

CHAPTER FIFTY FOUR

Forbidding Carib Sea Destruction Sunk

The virulent Pacho was gone, but filthy garbage barges continued. Kill one crook, hire another. We had seen the SPS port and determined the mission they had for the corporations in Texas. Vanna had been spinning her wheels and bouncing ideas off me. We finally went to face Brearly.

He was a new man. He had been excited by how the shrimp thieves were decimated. He looked back in command with a wink in his eye, never seen by us before. Bathing in pride his efforts made this happen. I brought up the barge mission, he stiffened.

We remembered very well how the thieves and U.S. government corruption had brought him to tears. Clear again, Vanna outlined the plan: a huge exercise needing timing and cooperation of people not closely related. I was hopeful, but fearful. Brearly felt he could easily perform his far-ranging part. A sigh of relief from me.

Vanna and I went back to our resort, an armory now. Zulinda had promised back-up if needed. Vanna, happy I had requested nothing from her, was designated to go to shore to sweet talk Songbird for his drone.

There were always hesitations in working with the big self-aggrandized buffoons above him. He was with us in spirit and needed us to ignore any actions we didn't understand that could come to pass in his support. They did come to pass, and we did ignore.

CHAPTER FIFTY FIVE

Payback

I was cog number three and never let her out of my sight. Troubling; she was under the barge several times for distant fin strokes. For port waters, there was decent visibility.

Brearly, Songbird, Vanna, and I, with drones, daily scanned the weather and the behavior of the barges and gunboats. The timings of departure of the three caravans were hard to read. They came clear. They steamed as to have one leaving the Texas port while another was dropping filth on the waters north of Orilla. The other was resting in SPS. The SPS gunboat steamed southwest to rip and dynamite huge swaths of life south and west of Orilla. Reversing north north-east it avoided the one coming into Orilla waters east from Texas. The third, having polluted Orilla had coordinated its rest time with the one in SPS. When the ripping started they'd cast off and follow the last to leave now being an hour north-east. When it came into sight east of Orilla, it decimated a swath parallel to the previous and headed straight north to a Texas corporation for a new pre-paid load.

While Brearly was registering thug trips, he came upon a constant, a period of time the Mekong River gunboats were repeating.

With fewer reconnaissance instruments to divert our thoughts, Vanna and I were doing more planning on What's App for an R&R in Munich. The map also showed the relatively short distances from Munich to Croatia's island of Rab. By Zoom, Cheryl warned: "It looks close now; any day after August twenty, you'll be driving through a mountain snowstorm worried to find a log resort to batten down for the night. Carry extra blankets, power bars and liquid."

Playing it down a little bit, Lance returned, "If and when anything happens, we'll keep it in mind. We have perhaps one of our most dangerous missions coming in a day or two. Birdcage out for now."

CHAPTER FIFTY SIX

Direct Contact

The first stage with possible direct contact was the most dangerous. We headed Octavio's boat, camouflaged, with Rayban and Zeren, to the SPS port. We left at 1:30 a.m. with no moon.

We anchored in the cat-tails and Vanna quickly took a satchel of limpet mines, other explosives and in plastic, a pistol with suppressor. She slipped under the water. I missed the wake of her rebreather. The Viet Nam gunboat command was asleep.

In the early morning wave-reflected sunlight, I couldn't see her for a nerve-stressing time. Suddenly she popped at the stern of the trawler, beckoning urgently to me. Warning Octavio, I slipped gently under the chop and swam hard underwater until I bumped her with my right hand.

She stayed in the water and pulled my ear close. "Lance, I'm sorry, I can't do this alone. Both the gunboat and the barge are too long for me to arm in one trip. I can do the gunboat and one on the barge. I need you to mount two more on the barge. I never meant to put you in this much danger. You'll have to swim with me, fix one of the limpets under the water line of the bow and another under the belly. I'll be longer; wait for me at the stern. Be careful not to float into me. I'll have the final mine for this group."

I affixed front limpet and reached to affix another. I couldn't reach the midpoint. I had to swim two quiet strokes over; quick back. I now understood what her difficulty had been.

I moved to the stern and tried to spot her, fending off any danger if it arose. I could see her struggling trying to reach with her arm to avoid breaking the surface. I thrust my hardened right elbow. She pushed off lunging to affix her third. She pounded, fins submerged to get back to me and out before trouble arrived. They could wake at any time. She tugged my hand dragging me three strokes until I got up to speed. We returned our escape under water, dampening any loud inhalation after our distance with no snorkel.

Sweating taking her mask off, it was not ocean water.

Tense, we heard the wailing and grinding of the two-some, gunboat and barge leaving. We burbled back toward Guanaja; at midpoint cranked to loud and fast.

Thirty per cent done. We placed the remote charges during the first rotation of the rusted craft, waiting. We had only five hours of sleep and had to go back. She gave me additional training. In a flash, I placed two on the front and middle of the barge again. She was right there with the third as I finished.

Brearly was going to have the Black suits with helicopters standing bye up on the Panhandle. Songbird had been cooperating. I'd be operating the drone with the third remote from Guanaja on the tower.

CHAPTER FIFTY SEVEN

Personal Danger

The personal danger was not over for Vanna, nor me. We relaxed and slept, so to speak, for two days. Dealing with danger is a major aphrodisiac. Our strong stress sweetly relieved, we slept.

Brearly stationed the black suits outside the Texas port. A day later, he hurriedly radioed, "This is the time. They're in normal traveling format."

Adrenaline surged again and I asked Vanna to inform Songbird. He said he could operate only within a mile of the shore.

"Officially! I wished those stinking Re's were sitting on the filthy barges."

We had to wait till twilight again for the third convoy to arrive. We had the drill down and were fast-in, but... not out. Limpets set, pounding away, I heard a muffled scream below the surface and blood was flowing from her left shoulder. I returned to assist and was hit in the calf, more blood. We grasped each other with the undamaged limbs wallowing to the boat. Now we had to depend on friends.

They were camouflaged. Rayban lifted Vanna effortlessly, a butterfly, and struggled with my straining wrists pulling me aboard. Zeren floored the Octavio to overdrive and headed north away from the port and west to the island suburb.

Bridge handed to Octavio, Zeren spun to deal with the

bleeding. Octavio kept looking over his shoulder to see if there were any fast boats in pursuit. A thirty-five horse aluminum poked its prow out of the fronds, no hope.

Vanna had no shrapnel inside her. Zeren quickly grasped my calf hurling a howl from me. She felt metal and grabbed the first aid kit for a forceps. I screamed again and it was out. She stayed with me temporarily tightening a tourniquet to stop the bleeding. She sprayed local anesthetic, the damage was not only on the outside. She turned back spraying, coating the drying blood on Vanna's back. She put antibiotic cream on Vanna causing her to freeze with a viscous growl. An angry huff as the bandage went on.

Zeren with command, "Sorry to you both, I know what I'm doing."

It took me a few minutes to snap out of shock. I remembered the other major actions under way. I struggled with the pain until I could move the leg and right myself. Zeren slammed me back down. I ignored her and asked, "Vanna, what's your sitrep?"

Dealing with a Seal, I got, "The spray anesthetic was the worst of it. I can move and don't think I'm bleeding much. It must have been a glancing blow off a rib. Zeren, I'm not bleeding much, right?"

Zeren, "Not much I can see under a tight bandage. I'm not going to dig it up to find out. Nobody is going to be ballet dancing off this boat tonight."

"Vanna, the injury is on your back, can you walk?"

"Lance, I can walk pretty well and know what you are trying to do. I agree to do it and can do it. You'll not be involved. Stay sensible! I know your piece of the puzzle, can walk to the drone, not carrying you, and coordinate with the other guys. Assuming the thugs haven't discovered our third set of limpets in SPS, we'll succeed with this."

Zeren blubbers at Vanna who says, "Zeren, I am beholden

for your capable care. You know I am a Seal and therefore I know my limits. I'm not stupid as to invite failure or serious additional injury. With a hole in his leg, Lance is in danger if he tries to fight his way up there. Tie him down if you have to. I will be leaving with no essence of ballet. I'll be in touch every step of the way."

CHAPTER FIFTY EIGHT

Coordinated Reprisal

No congressional derelicts counted on the hit they would take from the impending loss of dark campaign money. They would laugh off the pain I anticipated to endure. My back burn was within my pain tolerance. No feeling of bleeding. I took Lance's Orilla track. Brearly was on the Island. His troops hidden on the Texas coast.

We had set watches according to the three time zones. A single touch of a remote by each of us;..... down before they could talk to each other or anyone else.

Brearly made the call that shook the Island. I responded in tandem. Time dragging on for me, I heard Songbird.

Brearly had eyes on the sea outside the Texas harbor. Mission: nobody lives to tell the tale. His drone saw little left from the limpets. Blew another hole in each craft to guarantee rapid sinking.

I pushed off on my cell phone and looked to the drone picture. Orilla was in the background, the reef ripper was imploding taking the barge gasping down with it. A thug roused at the front of the barge. A piece of metal from the ripper down with the wreck. A far quicker death than he deserved after the continuous torture he had caused. The water was three hundred feet deep. The location was far from swimmable to Orilla. Their total loss.

Songbird was last to push his remote device. I guess he was waiting to see if we would really do this. On the other hand, he had extended his mentioned wavelength and took the third rusted crafts a mile off the SPS coast. A floating inferno of fire.

Afterwards, and with a few pain-killer Southern Comforts, Lance and Vanna mused, "Few decent humans in the world would be aware of a caravan of cartel thugs annihilated near Central America. The bribed congressmen from Texas surely did. No garbage Don J. Mondo was ever held accountable. They would lose their big election cartel campaign monies. This time!" (Lempiras)

They could damage my career and ability to personally manage my life's investment, the Starr Resort. Not in a court dealing with the truth. There was no evidence; no corpus delecti. However, they owned the courts.

CHAPTER FIFTY NINE

Finally Inevitable

Vanna was down for only ten days. With a hole in the leg not hitting bone, I moved little and slow for three weeks. Both Zeren and Vanna were my doctors. I didn't have to gamble with a Cartel one on the coast or an ungodly expensive one in the U.S. A bullet wound raises other unanswerable questions. I was tight-rope pushing in opposition, travel to Canada was significant.

CHAPTER SIXTY

On Rab Again After Twenty Years

With Vanna strong and me reduced to a slight limp, we headed to Munich and points beyond. We had deep conversations with Cheryl along with unexpectedly precise advice from Greg. We borrowed their Mercedes and drove on to Croatia and the ferry to Rab.

The island, part of Croatia, was thirty miles in diameter. Several dive operations were in existence. We had corresponded with the one on the market, but visited several others. Pricing a foreigner was a joy because we were moving into a culture where over-charging innocents was the way of doing business. I had been there twenty years before and that would not be part of a culture that would change any time soon. Not unaware! Beyond that, we learned snippets of important local marketing information. The two most important snippets were the clientele were from Southern Europe with some from Croatia and the countries no longer called Yugoslavia. The other fact was the diving was not much for rich reefs. Wrecks from the late 1800's through the Second World War were the fascination. Man-made reefs were in process in the area. In the cold water they'd take longer than any developer would live.

We were now prepared to begin dealing with the seller of the listed resort. An old guy who could be a brother of Brearly met us. Same rough weathered skin and eyes with no nonsense attitude. Borna, afraid of nothing, much less foreigners, was welcoming but distant. His wife, Anika was and had been the relationship builder keeping friend and strangers at ease. Borna was in his middle sixties fit with rippled shoulders, but weakness beginning to show the awful crush of aging. Anika was ten years younger, still in her prime, still his young love. Both gifted with such life. Down on the boat dock were two young bucks manhandling the dive boats and tanks.

Borna started, "Lance, and Donya Vanna, if I may, welcome to the resort, Horvats's History. It was an active resort forty years ago in our youth. It has continued to be profitable except for the years of the downturn of the destruction and division of the Yugoslavian Peninsula."

It's back now, even better. The only reason I've tentatively put it on the market is the increased help I need from the two you see on the dock. I'm fighting age the best I can. I'm aware. Anika, mine, doesn't make a peep.

I'm not decrepit and still need, for emotional balance, some labor within my comfort zone. At this age, things could change unexpectedly. Therefore, I sell the resort with the understanding you will technically be the owners. I will work within my limits and consult when years of experience put me in the know. My salary expectations will continue. As I will retire with social security pensions, they won't be high. You will soon find my salary in the gross costs will not hinder other operations or development.

His requests were clearly understood and although we were on the verge of entering the middle years, with those young guys on the dock, we could easily handle the operations for several years longer.

With the mentioned priorities on the table, we discussed an offer related to the sale of Starr Resort to Roberto.

CHAPTER SIXTY ONE

Heart-Felt Partings

Arriving back in Guanaja, we had set a path. The complicated changes, soul-searching and heartbreak hit each of us.

The deepest pain for me was leaving a business I had built from the very jungle floor. What I had seen for sale in Rab, there was a future in my field, with Vanna's share consistent. We were out of the clutches of the worst corruption in the U.S. We paid U.S. taxes only on monies above the $80,000 per person per year overseas deduction. Uncommitted up to $160,000, we had American Passports which gave us the background to settle most anywhere in the West. The passport no longer had the power and unblemished respect it had before Trump. Some foreigners had approached me to say they were sorry for what I, as an American, had now. Sentiments of several people in several countries identical.

Nobody else in our group could easily go and get a work permit in another country. Deep family issues boded. An overwhelming concern for Vanna and I was the idea of going and leaving two defensive positions open.

Roberto was Honduran and Cindy held a work permit for Honduras, a Peruvian Passport. They had family and business issues nor did they want to walk north and face the Trump Stockade at the border. The bright spot was they didn't have to pay U.S. taxes.

At the same time, Alicia was losing her grip keeping the cartel from again threatening restaurant owners and their families. The rows and ditches of Central America were festering scores, hundreds of these mind-altered thugs. An army would be hard pressed to bring back any order. Vanna had had to save my life many times and I hers. if we wanted to survive, and odds were against it, it couldn't be here.

CHAPTER SIXTY TWO

Unimpeded Warnings

Vanna and I were analyzing what our most empathetic actions needed be with Roberto. As an original part owner, the future of the resort ultimately fell to him and Cindy.

Sea rescue radio blared, Blearly hoarsely reported, "The thugs on my island here, which is yours, Roberto, are gathering between you and Half Moon Bay Resort. I only see Cindy there holding the onslaught on the barbed wire fence. You better get there stat, set up the new armory you got from Zulinda and get between her and danger. She only has an automatic. It won't carry a breath in this windstorm. I'll have a few of my security snipe them from a distance, you need the Gatling."

We jumped out of our bungalow and Roberto raced for his inboard. Vanna and I grabbed weapons and ammo as much as we could carry. Vanna called Zulinda to locate Octavio and Zeren. I called a boat captain to volunteer help. Rayban had an argument about Zeren coming and immediately lost it. They roared to the west end of Zulinda's beach and gathered more weapons and ammo. Zulinda, panting and womanly bouncing to the stash said, "Lance, while you were in Germany, we had some trouble here. As a result, and due to his shrimp farm's small barbed wire fence, I gave Roberto a Gatling gun to protect Cindy. He has it camouflaged on his back porch, You need to bring packs and packs of ammunition. I'll help load. Octavio, awash with armory, Vanna on the front deck shifted weight ahead to bring the bow down lifting the engine up to secure the plane-off. Speed enhanced our 23 knots by seven.

Roberto ran his whole cruiser up his sand beach leaping off with two submachine guns racing to find Cindy and get her behind him. She was on one knee firmly and deliberately knocking down thugs on the fence. If it weren't dangerous it could be a shooting gallery in a carnival. Bodies piling up.

Roberto hugged her back to the porch where they had practiced mounting the gun. They had burrowed slits in the bottom of the wall to insert the legs. The recoil didn't knock them up against the house. In the delay for set-up, several thugs got into the yard. Cindy rammed in the first magazine; Roberto cleared the yard of crawling demons. They appear like cockroaches. He focused again on the fence.

The whole group of Starr Resort protectors initially had discussed trying to defend; not use offensive procedures. Our civilized attempts at rules of engagement soon ended with a shot fired or some another attack obvious and looming. Yard clear, Roberto paused, letting the creatures decide their fate. A roar of filth erupted from a lieutenant in the forest behind the sniveling mob. A rush for the fence with explosions and fire, the bodies now fell on the opposite side of the fence.

Cindy shouted, "We only have a half dozen clips left."

Roberto, "Listen honey, Octavio will be here before we run out. Can't you hear his cruiser coming in planed-off?"

Cindy, anxious, "We didn't get earplugs for this monster, I can't even hear my heartbeat, and believe me, it's racing."

Lance, loaded with arms and ammunition swerved around the left corner to the porch. Vanna on his right protecting him, firing accurately; a new cleansing of the fence. Zeren couldn't get in front of Rayban, no way, and came loping behind him while he unloaded scores of clips next to Cindy. Bido, the boat captain was the last to arrive his machine gun on full report. Two women and three men left scores of bodies on both sides of the fence. The fighting paused, the boat captain fired off a final fuselage hitting three interlopers, and the rest whined into the woods with the lieutenant screaming trying to force them back. An ugly quiet fell on the yard. Octavio and the boat captain surged ahead to dispose of the bodies to the other side of the fence.

CHAPTER SIXTY THREE

The Sorry Dismantling

The team pulled chairs inside up to the door. Roberto, still on the Gatling, could hear.

Lance immediately took lead. "Roberto, I'm sorry, you are not selling enough shrimp to risk your two lives here. They will burn you out in a matter of days. As we discussed, as part owner of Starr, we will sell it to you at approximately half of actual value. We need the other to set up shop on Rab. You will remain very financially viable. I don't know what to say to Alicia. You'll have to decide according to your agreement. Vanna and I have already talked to Blearly and Maria. They aren't going anywhere. It's in their interest to have a pro scuba diving resort located near their island. With them, you know it isn't only about money. They'll bend the rules of their board to protect you."

From the porch, Roberto jumped in, "Octavio, Starr will continue our protection for your Caribbean businesses. United we'll stand".

Lance hurries, "We have to absolutely, immediately, get you and Cindy out of here. Give me the Gatling and you two and Vanna get your belongings packed with waterproof wrapping where possible. Boat captain, "Bido, we can't leave these people alone after dark. Take the security boat back, get the other captains and bring all boats including the ramps back. Go quickly, run it as fast as you can handle it. It'll churn 35 knots without damage."

The house became quiet with the sounds of packing and quiet tears when a treasure had to be abandoned. Lance concentrated on the fence at setting sun. Vanna helped with packing, mostly standing near him pegged to the Gatling. When they are in danger, they are invariably back to back, eyes burning with radar precision. Looking sadly into the distance Lance called Roberto and Cindy over to his perch.

Lance, quietly, "it's going to feel forever waiting for the ramp boats. We need to take a minute to decide how we handle Starr. I can't avoid all heart break. I will run a plan by you, accept changes at any time. We'll be ready to organize upon arrival. Vanna and I will need a day to pack and clear our stuff out of what will become your bungalow if you wish. Tonight, you and Cindy take one of the full service bungalows. We'll leave the household goods on the boats."

"Octavio, could you and Zeren either come up and sleep in a bungalow or sleep on your cruiser tonight. I'm leery about what these louts might dream up after losing scores of their underlings. I want to be as close to full defense mode as we can."

"Vanna, do you think Phil, in banana operations is still there at this time?"

"They have a train every day at dark. He'll be there for a couple hours at least."

"Ok, see how soon he can get a skiff out. We'll pay all, and take our house-hold goods and security boat to the next banana boat going empty to Europe. Ask the help of two pickers but keep it as confidential as possible. I don't want Donny J. to get wind of this and seek sickly advantage. Tell him there will be two automatic weapons and ammunition."

At exactly sunset, two misshapen animalistic faces jumped up on the fence to test for another attack. As they jumped, they were blown back onto the Half-Moon bay resort impaled on a fence post. No movement. Lance didn't even look down at Vanna reloading her rifle.

The waiting dragged on and it was one in the morning the ramp boats rumbled in. Loading with minimum lights, they rolled out again at 3 a.m.

It took two days to get the skiff pick-up. We had our last loving and bubbles in the Caribbean.

"Well, let's review", said Lance.

For Starr, Roberto brought his cousin full time as diver and island defense. They need one more. He has not had time to request the FBI clearances. He and Cindy also had dinner with Brearly and Maria to confirm further support and any prohibitions. Soon there will be a journey to United Fruit area veterinary to plan a future with Alicia. Josh is now handling the drone in coordination with Blearly's Black Bird and Octavio's trips north. Juan and the Railroad Street Regulars have shifted their protective services to Roberto. Bucky came back to Guanaja living with Roberto and Cindy.

Schedules conflicted and we needed to wait another day to fly to Frankfurt and on to Croatia.

We took snorkels down to the East end on the sand. We experienced some of the elation Trey and Fran felt as they fell in love there. Vanna was a woman with whom I could repeatedly fall in love, and did!

CHAPTER SIXTY FOUR

Rab, The Rest From Stress?

Roberto, my friend since university dorm days had been supportive, self-effacing. From money, not a hint of braggadocio, fearless in defense of the resort and protective of all. Self-confidence varied. He endured bravely to support his now wife, Cindy, through a disease she got in Nepal. No doctor, at least in Spain, could identify or treat. On the other hand, he left feeling shame when Vanna had taken all four cartel goons down in the camp Mondo attack and he had not gotten a shot off.

Shy, yet sophisticatedly proper, you'd never guess Roberto came from a serious financial family in Honduras. He was staying in the most luxurious dorm room in our building. His hall could house three double units. He had two of those renovated into one with more chairs, beds, and desks. He was generous if Greg or I had a beauty we wanted to impress. He took most of a spring break searching for a site for my scuba resort and at the same time bought a shrimp farm and dolphin riding concession. His father agreed he could take a year off after graduation to do the famous backpacking trip across Europe. As recounted in Book I, Cindy short-circuited the trip in Spain.

He developed close friendships with Greg and I and the guy who was living in what was the remaining one third of his hallway. From Croatia, he was the furthest from home in our complex. Surprisingly, Marko was also the best basketball player. Greg and I double-dated and at times Marko and Roberto shared a view of their lovelies. He was here due to the reputation of the school in Marine studies. After graduation Marko and Roberto maintained their acquaintance via skype and Zoom. With Roberto frequenting the development of the Starr Professional Diving Resort, I often joined in the repartee and learned more about Croatia and specifically Rab. Marko had never been to Rab, although he was a certified, infrequent diver. I had been there before the horrible clash in and around Serbia. Marko and I had that connection and he was surprised and pleased we were going to take over a diving resort. Roberto kept him informed about the terrible fate of Hondurans and the serious affect it had had on his shrimp farm and Dolphin riding concession. He recounted his now new ownership of Starr Resort.

CHAPTER SIXTY FIVE

Rab, The Inexplicable Introductions

Marko was there at Rijeka Airport to pick us up and escort us through Istria and onto the Rab Ferry to the island. It was about 25 kilometers by Ferry. I planned to buy a car once there. Marko would lead us by the hand through the red tape of buying a local car. It needed to happen soon. With an exchange of 15 local currency, Kuna, to a dollar and the generous proceeds from the sale of the resort, we quickly bought high power, low gas. Frankly, I bought formidable, not quite a tank, because if Vanna ever got into a collision, I wanted her to have as much metal as possible between her and the intruder. We also anticipated some transport of divers. We knew of the 2023 change to the Euro, which would make our purchase in dollars, much more expensive.

Marko took his car onto the ferry to the island of the resort. At the ferry, we were early going for the fresh breezes from the Adriatic. I saw in dreadful slow motion something I had seen once in Greece and expected never to see again in this lifetime. The boat was full except the last car row. There was a metal plate affixed to the dock and a similar plate on the back of the boat. While docked, the two plates overlapped so cars could drive on and at the destination back off. While underway the boat's ramp was raised. The one on the dock was delayed in closing a few seconds each time to raise a more structural steel barricade. The ferry was raising steam for the path across to the island. Both the ramps were still down. A guy in a Lada sedan came barreling over the small ridge which marked the parking area for the ferry. I couldn't imagine what part of his brain was fomenting this absolute stupidity. He didn't slow and hit the shore ramp before it had raised. The boat's ramp was still down, had pulled away a few feet from the shore. He floored it to jump the distance, ramp still down; then brake. Front wheel drive, weight in the front, the nose plunged causing the two front tires to slam the ramp steel now rising. They exploded leaving the metal wheels to bear the brunt of the front bumper of the car and then the radiator. Up in the air soared the front body of the car causing a perfect rear summersault. It landed on its roof and pressure inside the car exploded throwing the driver out. After his shock, his eyes flared, he couldn't swim. If you ever see the eyes of a drowning person, you have no doubt. Flailing, the guy was delirious. I am more than a professional life guard and absolutely would not to get close to a guy in this condition. I grabbed one of the boat's yellow floating rings, threw it back to Marko at the rear and he threw it on to the man. The guy wasn't lucid and didn't even see it or know it was there. Marko quickly retrieved the ring and this time threw it right at his head. The guy flailed again and touched it, hugging it closely to his chest. Marko reeled the guy in and before he could stand him up, the Captain throttled him by the neck, dragging him up to the pilot house. I heard the engines pause, a dingy was floated out from the lower stern deck. The First Mate man-handled Mr. Russian, late owner of one Lada, into it and rowed him back to the dock. Leaving the lawyers to fight the obvious, the captain hit full flank throttle, not looking back. The Police were there. I looked at Vanna. We shook our heads.

CHAPTER SIXTY SIX

A Civil Challenge

Rab had developed rapidly during the twenty years I had been away. Where there had been sheep-filled rocky fields, buildings and high rise hotels lined the beaches. One of the dive resorts got such an offer for their beach front, they retired and closed. Three were left, mine and two others.

The little Bed and Breakfast where only brackish water had been available, salty coffee had been a non-starter. The hosts were so uncomfortable, they gave me Slivovitz as my liquid to start the day. It was a high start. The folks had been well beyond retirement and now, the old house was no longer there.

Borna and Anika were out to meet us, surly and sweet. Marko had never met them. There was a few minutes of Croatian give and take. Dead tired from jet lag, I urged all hands to get our suitcases. We sent Marko on his way with a promise to join him and his fiancé for dinner within a week. I corrected the timing to wait one day for every hour we gained in lag.

After four days, we woke and christened our new, and safer, love nest. There were two temporarily heated heart beats and back to doze until evening and full sleep again. We woke the next day to hunger.

Two more days getting time arranged to local zones and we swam off the dock. Evidently, Marko was counting the days and called in with the dinner invite.

I responded, "ok, but let's look for a truck for Vanna before the Kuna evolves into the Euro."

Marko came alone; "took us to the dealership with the largest selection. I asked about bargaining. He said, "Absolutely, let me do it. They take tourists for a ride."

I was satisfied with a 20% reduction and we drove in tandem back to Horvatz, my resort. Maybe we need to think about another name.

We took Marko down to the dock to discuss the quality of the equipment and found Borna hadn't skimped. Marko agreed to join us for an introductory dive on the weekend.

Dinner day, we went up and dressed. Vanna was going eye-hunting. The visions she provided me, purchased in Frankfurt, surely granted permission. She should be illegal, but the restaurant was ritzy and romantic. We had seen pictures of the fiancé and an eye duel was possible. Thirty seconds after Petra met Vanna it could be ruled out. Here was a younger version of the welcoming personality of Anika.

Chemistry was sweet and accepting both ways. The only ogle eyes were mine. I need to hide carefully or wear very dark glasses at all times. I was careful and can professionally say, "Petra looked good enough to eat without sauce."

There was no dearth of things to talk about. Notably Petra was more of a diver than Marko, to which he embarrassingly agreed. The other surprise, and I shouldn't have been, was the wedding was booked for five weeks away. We were invited, of course, but the court was and should be composed of their friends who had been with them for scores of years.

The most stressful event happened when a well-oiled local in the restaurant fell for Vanna. He was to my left and Vanna's right. He started moving our way and I could read the vodka and lust in his eyes. Vanna read mine and turned shoulders square to his. The bouncer had seen the eyes. Two steps and he took him hard to the floor knocking his wind out avoiding any close call to Vanna.

Only I realized how close to impending death this guy would

be if he got close to her. There would be broken chairs and bones in five seconds. She wouldn't even be breathing heavily.

Neither Marko nor Petra reacted, nor realized; they didn't know she was a Seal. Our table hadn't been compromised so I quickly ordered another round of drinks and shifted back to the wedding. Nuptials to be thirty feet under water near the vertical cliffs of the Adriatic beside Kvarnar Bay.

Smiling, Marko put us in the picture, or whatever picture he had heard painted from a guide when he was ten.

"The main attraction is the sand beach. South-east past the peninsula stand the vertical cliffs which extend underwater to walls, caves and caverns. They have been here for eons and their protrusion provides a seafloor meandering out to a hundred fifty feet, thirty to fifty feet deep. It drops off fast visibility literally goes black. At a depth of 300 feet hangs the hulk of a boat dating back to the Greeks. Sport diving is limited to 120 feet. Little is known of whatever crumbling may be left. Local "bar-flies" and colorful guides spin most interesting tales of the provenance of the ships in the area. With many areas to choose, we decided to be conservative and locate the ceremony where the water was about thirty feet deep. Tank time necessary would put the tanked diving guests in no danger of "the bends" or "nitrogen narcosis".

A sparkling story to end our first date on Rab. Vanna drove us home in her tank offering to present various activities she also enjoyed done at thirty feet.

The date marked the end of "jet lag". We eagerly awaited Borna's tour to create our illusion as knowledgeable locals. To a novice, grueling, between the myths and tall tales he recounted, he stopped and put us through shallow dives.

With a subtle and infrequent sense of humor, his seriousness resounded that his resort maintain its quality reputation. Thus we did an additional two days of introductory ten foot dives learning the whole area. Finally, with caution in his voice, he took us down to 180 feet for ten minutes. On a regular tank, you only stay at 100 feet for ten minutes. No decompression at 10 feet required. He had chosen his newest tanks and loaded them with 3,500 psi rather than 3,000. He was going to decide if we were what we said we were. He would soon find I wasn't a novice.

For Vanna, this was way below her expertise. She had been diving frequently, so deep she had to decompress three times for extended waits. Fifteen minutes at 60 feet and 10 minutes at ten feet, was no chore for her. I didn't have the hours of experience she had. When I first opened the Starr Resort, I quickly learned the dangers of the area and ventured down to 200 feet in several locations. I was prepared for any hot-shots trying to push the sport-diver limits. The future of my investment assured, I was more than ready.

We dawdled around ten minutes with Borna and I called the surface warning. We surfaced no faster than our bubbles and Vanna called the decompression at sixty feet. We stayed fifteen minutes. At ten feet, I stopped us for another ten. We surfaced with no pain nor pressure. I had the feeling of two hot pokers ramming my back as Borna's eyes analyzed my every move. I saw him judge Vanna, quickly realizing what he had here. We left the water shedding our tanks. Borna was looking ugly at us and broke into a seldom seen smile. I passed and she more than passed.

In tandem, Vanna and I went three times on every dive trip to every used location. We did three separated between ramp boats with a muscled boy watching. We were ready to handle any dive and to assign the muscle boys where we wanted them, no whining.

CHAPTER SIXTY SEVEN

Our Personal Self-Orientation

Satisfied with our skill and people relations, Borna stepped back and as promised, only came out to answer questions not obvious in a new resort and culture. If we had a sick bruiser, he'd cover for him for the day.

Soon after we had been receiving a good number of divers, more than covering the costs, Anika came out with an unanticipated spark in her eye.

Smiling, she continued, "I know you are coming from the Caribbean with lots of experiences probably with South American Cultures and many U.S. divers. Not many Europeans, I guess."

Vanna answered, "A few. I've seen from marketing efforts, you target mostly southern Europe. A problem?"

Anika continues, "No problem. Maybe we've been here so long we don't notice. From diving pictures on the internet and other sources, most everybody in the Caribbean wears a suit or a wet suit. The comparative word here is liberal, the majority of women wear nothing or only a bottom. The water here is more salty and, at depth, cooler than the Caribbean. Wet suits are needed by most all divers. The wet suit comes off; there is seldom anything left. Maybe you come from a more conservative background or haven't seen much of this over there. Maybe it will be a problem for you. I need to make sure you understand this dress is ingrained in the European and Eastern Block cultures we serve. If you should criticize or insult anyone, man or woman or child about this, they will be shocked, angered and never repeat a vacation with us. Such a failure will be big news and we'll be in trouble, probably bankrupt in one year."

"Anika, Vanna answers, we appreciate the "heads-up". Far away as we are, conservative mores in the U.S., are not followed by a majority. Thongs that wouldn't cover a 2 Euro coin compete. We saw a variety."

"At the same time, and I appreciate it if you keep this between us, I am a retired Navy Seal and have served in a myriad of cultures. I entered the Seal Organization when women were first accepted. The colleagues I associated with were close to all men. I took more showers in the presence of men than not. I am not inhibited nor is Lance. If proper, we could well be out on the boat or the beach attired, or "not attired" as you see. We really appreciate your care in informing us. If this should be the biggest problem having a resort here, how happy we will be."

Lance continues, "Anika, this'll not be a problem with us. However, there are surely values and mores in your culture more subtle. Don't hesitate to keep us informed as we go along."

CHAPTER SIXTY EIGHT

Business Once Usual, Nights Free Of Threats

For a while, we carried idling stress with us. Sometimes a dream. The resort was well-marketed and the two Hercules males warmed up and respectful relationships developed. The hellish memories faded. We added a new cook losing the experienced one to a Michelin Five Star on the mainland. A mixed drink person to boot. Croatia, once part of Yugoslavia divided into the wealthiest of splinter states. Tourism was twenty per cent of the export national income. Here we were right in the middle.

The Adriatic is salty making it possible for even lead-footed swimmers to float. On the other hand, it is the coolest finger off the Mediterranean. A lot of Alps-driven melts find their way and keep the water cool even in the height of summer. The large number of sunny days year-round create a mix of cool water temperatures most of the year. Wet suits are frequent even above the thermo-clime.

The comparatively bitter cold of Europe drives people south even in winter months. Wet suits with this group are only suggested. Look out across the sand on a comparatively cool or rainy day and listen for the language of the group whooping it up. Eight of ten times it will be German.

Spring came early and the bus tours and cars flowed in from the North. As forewarned, the beaches swarmed with women in small or no attire. Only the diver women wore wet suits, femininely cut, one-quarter inch thick. Curves kept warm.

Vanna is strikingly beautiful and had no competition, but for self-protection, I kept my head down when busts appeared........ When she was watching!

CHAPTER SIXTY NINE

Society's Liberal Weddings At 30 Feet

Weather cooperated up to the Big Week; the decision was made thirty feet down, no wave affect. Along with the wedding group, several couples including Vanna and I dove to the depth of the vows.

In the environment, surely a cultural thing, I laughed out bubbles. The wedding party men had wet suits with trappings of a tuxedo in decals affixed in correct location all over the black insulating texture; including cumber bun and bow-tie. Formal underwater apparel. Amusement was mild, then, breathtaking:

Down came the bridesmaids, wet-suit cleavages exposed over remnants of material on long flowing dresses. Not a bloomer culture. They frolicked and spun sending sheets of color out and up around their Victoria Secret carved waists. A repeating flurry of booty color. A phosphorescent sunrise of emigrating multi-colored jelly fish surging to sandy beaches?

We are in nude beach international. 'Default' nude. Not nude, except… One eighth inch wetsuit material Victoria Secret cut. Garter belts and lingerie some opaque, some less, a few bikinis. Stocking tops. Many not in the wedding party were less attired, much less, providing cleavages with no wet suit, stimulation too much for any male to ignore Closed, for descending, the dresses were wrapped by small velcro straps holding them to thighs to enter the water. Once the legs were flexed, Velcro slipped under the dress belt to be tucked into the arm-sleeves.

After exactly three minutes of manic panorama, velcro re-fit; colors muted, Petra, with scheduled delay, began her descent above Marko. Velcro refused. A most seductive cultural tradition. As the bride descended, her dress floated up around her presenting the most alluring vision uniquely for him. The bride, most captivating of all. Her day, his capture! Absolutely fitting!

As the diver minister moved to be flanked by Marko and Petra, women closed, only Petra's color remained. The words were heard on ear-buds under-water rescue radios and names were signed on a sharpie tablet.

CHAPTER SEVENTY

Catastrophe

As a few people began to ascend, a blast of huge proportions thundered out from the wall. People flying in all directions, many in fetal lock. The surge of water pushed me back. The bubbles in the water pelting every inch of my body. I saw the power of the surge and Vanna forced herself around and in front of me to buffer the turmoil. A personal flak jacket. Her fingers vice-gripped my underarms pulling herself up against me. The blast ended. The water displaced threw us over spinning, bowling pins, left and right, down hard. Yards. The shock hammered me. Suddenly I couldn't breathe. With eyes of a drowning victim, I searched for Vanna. My regulator torn from my mouth was no longer connected to my tank. I lost lucidity. As Vanna was thrown toward concussion, she took her regulator and put it in my mouth. Huge breath, I weakly pushed it back. Every dive instructor in every scuba course pounds buddy-breathing until it becomes a habit. Breaking waves threw us uncontrolled to a spot on a black beach. Where had the sunny thirty feet gone? Vanna still gripped and between breaths forced us toward the black. It was not a beach. It was the entrance to a sunless cavern. She lost me for a heartbeat and I hit my head on granite. My life went black.

Trudging with lightning strikes in her head, Vanna dragged Lance foot by foot toward the line in the cave wall showing the highest level of surf. She fought sleep. She knew she had a concussion; knew what to do. Her bleary eyes stopped her motion trying to put her to sleep. She fought and rolled on her back pulling Lance's head up onto her midriff. He was motionless. She turned herself 90 degrees to him. She laid her head on his chest. The heartbeat was weak. She moved her arms up under his head, put the left under the neck and the right above the eyes. She moved her lips down to check his breathing. There was none. Thus the slowing heart function. She raised back, forgetting to check his airway, and brought her thumb and finger down to close his nose. Suddenly realized, in her fog, she hadn't checked for blockage. She released his nose and kept his neck up, checking his mouth. There was something. Keeping the neck back, she moved two fingers in to grasp whatever was there. The rough spiraling stem of an ancient reef plant, lodged deep. She closed her thumb and first finger. In her painful hurry, broke it off somewhere at his epiglottis. She went back with fingers on both hands, located the bristly thing and ever consistently removed it. Forever long. It had gone down either the esophagus or the throat. Lack of breathing suggested the former. As quickly as she could stretch her screaming muscles, she returned the block to his nose, and her breath to rescue breathing. Her brain was showing mist and trying to put her to sleep. She couldn't succumb. Her lips met his. He lurched, throwing his head hard left and right. She got out of the way. The ocean left him.

Flashing micro-seconds, thinking cleared: was this a lost sea mine from WWII, something vengeful against Marko, an explosive from the break-up of Yugoslavia, or some sick cartel lieutenant coming half way across the world to wreak vengeance on him? Comatose, he fell to her midriff. She slipped backwards, losing focus on raging bubbles, unable to fight sleep any longer, sliding into unwelcome darkness.

END GUANAJA DEFENSE BOOK TWO

www.ingramcontent.com/pod-product-compliance
Lightning Source LLC
Chambersburg PA
CBHW030146010826
48973CB00002B/753